F

S

DANGER IN THE NIGHT. . .

WILLIAM PAUSED, made certain of the watchman's course, hurried on—then froze. Footsteps were coming! Panicked, he flattened himself against a recessed shop door and seconds later sensed a moving human presence inches away: Bootheels sounded, clothing rustled, the faint breeze from the walker's passage brushed against his face. He heard a man's voice, humming jauntily.

Mr. Baggot, the tithingman! William's heart boomed. Even though he'd excused the apprentice from his twice-weekly examinations, the man had been much on William's mind. Twice he'd thought he'd glimpsed him lurking outside Mr. Currie's after dark, waiting to snare him, as he'd vowed to do. "I want you to know that my eye is upon you." His words reverberated in William's mind. . . .

SATURNALIA

Also by Paul Fleischman

The Birthday Tree
Coming-and-Going Men
Graven Images
The Half-A-Moon Inn
Path of the Pale Horse
Rear-View Mirrors
I Am Phoenix
Joyful Noise
Rondo in C
Copier Creations

SATURNALIA

by Paul Fleischman

A Charlotte Zolotow Book

HarperKeypoint
An Imprint of HarperCollins*Publishers*

Saturnalia
Copyright © 1990 by Paul Fleischman
Typography by Joyce Hopkins

Library of Congress Cataloging-in-Publication Data
Fleischman, Paul.
    Saturnalia / by Paul Fleischman
        p.   cm.
    "A Charlotte Zolotow book."
    Summary: In 1681 in Boston, fourteen-year-old William, a Nar-
raganset Indian captured in a raid six years earlier, leads a produc-
tive and contented life as a printer's apprentice but is increasingly
anxious to make some connection with his Indian past.
    ISBN 0-06-021912-2. — ISBN 0-06-021913-0 (lib. bdg.)
    ISBN 0-06-447089-X (pbk.)
    [1. Boston (Mass.)—History—Colonial period, ca. 1600–1775—
Fiction. 2. Narraganset Indians—Fiction. 3. Indians of North
America—Fiction. 4. Apprentices—Fiction. 5. Prejudices—
Fiction.] I. Title.
PZ7.F59918Sat 1990   89-36380
[Fic]—dc20   CIP
                                                        AC

HarperKeypoint is an imprint of Harper Trophy, a division of
HarperCollins Publishers. First Harper Keypoint edition, 1992.

For Ivy Ruckman

SATURNALIA

ONE

☀

T HE WEATHERVANES OF BOSTON were pointed north—the frigates, the angels, the cocks, the cows— and so, below, was Mr. Baggot. Marching down a dim alleyway, he raised his eyes from the shin-deep snow and gazed with envy at a rooftop rooster. The wooden bird was perched high enough to be sunning itself in the first light of day. While he himself, mused Mr. Baggot, trudged along in perpetual darkness, walking the lightless lanes of sin, rooting out evil and blasphemy. Such was the life of a tithingman.

It was December of 1681 and tombstone-cracking cold. Having bested fifty previous winters, Mr. Baggot was undeterred by the freezing gust of wind scouring his face and strode powerfully ahead without pause, parting the gale with his hatchet nose. In one hand he carried a well-worn copy of *Spiritual Stepping-Stones for the Young.* In the other he carried the symbol of his office, a walnut staff knobbed at one end and bearing a fox's tail on the other. In fulfilling his duties at Sunday's church service, he'd banged the staff's knob on the doltish heads of a variety of squirming, whispering, laughing, face-making, Satan-claimed children, while waking no less than four dozing adults with a tickle of the foxtail. Following this, he'd used it to trip a pair of boys running from the meetinghouse, had reported two men for swearing and one for shamelessly splitting wood on the Sabbath, and yesterday, to his great disgust, had descended into the hellish waterfront taverns in search of disorderly patrons. How far this foul metropolis was from the paradise it had promised! A thought punctuated by the emptying, from above, of a chamber pot directly in his path.

He turned onto King Street and nearly collided with a scissors grinder pushing his wheel. Tinkers, broom makers, fishwives, and wood sellers all sent their cries toward the roof of Heaven. Horses, carts, and rumbling wagons shook the Devil from bed below. Mr. Baggot tramped on, his cloak flapping in the breeze so that he seemed to be constantly changing shape, as if made of black quicksilver. In the distance he glimpsed a pair of ships, sails full, leaving Boston harbor. Closer at hand, he spotted a shop sign in the shape of a book, and girded himself.

4

Like the town's other tithingmen, he had spiritual charge of ten families, noting with care their attendance at services and testing their children's knowledge of Scripture. Among the homes on his circuit, none distressed him like that of Charles Currie, printer, a man of great knowledge who seemed to prefer the companionship of his books on Sundays to that of his neighbors in church. And among the young under Mr. Currie's roof, none irked him like William, the printer's apprentice. Not because the boy failed to study, like most—but because he knew far too much.

Mr. Baggot entered the printer's front room, causing the shop's bell to tinkle softly. Waiting for his presence to be noted, he sniffed breakfast, heard talking farther within, glanced about at the books, papers, pins, and other sundries for sale, coughed conspicuously, took off his cloak, listened to an outburst of general merriment, and finally pounded his staff on the floor.

"Ah, good Mr. Baggot." Mr. Currie's round, reddish face appeared around a doorway. "You find us at breakfast. Will you take some bread and milk?"

"Bread and milk leave me hungry," Mr. Baggot replied sternly. "Feeding the soul is my object. Your children's ravenous ones, this morning."

Mr. Currie smiled faintly. "Allow me a moment to instruct their souls to fetch bowl and spoon." Turtlelike, he drew in his head, while Mr. Baggot wondered whether he'd been mocked. He felt his anger smoke, then ignite, ransacked his brains for some revenge on the man, and found himself staring at a calendar for

5

December on the wall. His eyes traveled down to the twenty-fifth and narrowed. In the printer's favor, Mr. Baggot had never known him—or any but a handful— to celebrate Christmas in any way, much less with the feasting, dicing, and drinking that marked that reeking day in England. However, the tithingman had heard tell that in this same month of the year Mr. Currie, out of his love for the ancient authors, imitated the Romans of old and observed a Saturnalia, a depraved, pagan festivity in which masters and servants traded places. Was this not far worse than Christmas reveling? The man, he noted, bore closer watching.

Mr. Currie returned, guided Mr. Baggot down a hall, past the printing room, into the house's living quarters, and left him at a long bench near the hearth upon which perched six children of assorted heights.

"Now then." Mr. Baggot removed the hat from his wispy, wind-tormented red hair and straightened himself to his full six feet. His staff in one hand, he opened his book with the other and paced before the bench.

"Sarah. Who was the oldest man?"

"Methuselah," stated a confident voice.

"James. Who was the most patient man?"

"Job," came the reply.

"Timothy. Who was the most hard-hearted man?"

"Judas," lisped Mr. Currie's youngest son.

The tithingman rapped his head with his staff. "Pharaoh!" he corrected. "As sure as you're the most hard-*headed* boy in all Boston!"

Mr. Baggot paced, stopping before William, Mr. Cur-

6

rie's fourteen-year-old apprentice. He was tall and thin as a spring shoot, growing up through and out of his black breeches and white shirt. The tithingman stared at him in silence. How very English he looks, he reflected. A wig on his head, stockings on his calves, pewter-buckled shoes on his feet. How avidly he reads. How well he speaks. How universally admired he is. And how black is his barbarous heart, he added. For beneath his linen shirt and his Latin, the viper wasn't English. He was an Indian.

Mr. Baggot felt the boy's mere presence blow upon his wrath like a bellows. He noticed an exhibition piece of his penmanship mounted on the wall and thought of his own two tiny grandsons. They'd been too young to hold a pen when they were slain in their beds by savages, just before the end of the Indian war that had brought William to Boston as a captive. The tithingman ground his yellowed teeth. What had inspired Mr. Currie to send the tawny to school, to hire tutors, to read to him from Homer and Plato until his learning surpassed Mr. Baggot's own? No matter. Today he would humble the demon! He smiled knowingly, studied William's eyes, then moved on without a question.

"Rachel. Describe your condition in Hell."

"I shall be dreadfully tormented," came the memorized answer.

"Ruth. What company will you have there?"

"Legions of devils and multitudes of sinners."

"Timothy. Will company afford you comfort?"

"It will not," Mr. Currie's son lisped, "but . . ."

He halted. His clasped hands gripped each other. "But will surely . . ." His eyes appealed to the ceiling.

"*But will surely increase your woes!*" the tithingman finished the sentence for him, and increased the boy's present store of woes by the amount of two sharp raps on the head.

There followed several more minutes of drilling, Mr. Baggot passing over William each time. He next asked to examine the older children's notes taken on Sunday's sermon, and was saddened to see that the three-hour oration had left so little trace in their notebooks. He then offered them his weekly exhortations: to pray alone in secret places, to pray unceasingly, even during sleep, to rip sin from their souls, root and stalk. He walked toward the door with his book and staff, then turned.

"One question more."

He stared at William and half believed he'd fixed his gaze on the black eyes and bronze skin of his grandchildren's murderer.

"Do you think it just that one of you has answered no questions this morning?" he asked.

At once, William spied the man's scheme. "Grievously unjust!" he declared. "Put me any question you choose!" He wouldn't let the tithingman turn the others against him.

"Grievously unjust, indeed." Mr. Baggot searched hopefully for signs of resentment toward the apprentice.

"Though why should we fret if he's been favored?"

spoke up Sarah, the printer's eldest daughter. "Is that not just what Jesus taught in the story of the laborers in the vineyard?"

William smiled discreetly at this brilliant outflanking maneuver.

"Matthew, chapter twenty," added one of Mr. Currie's sons.

"Silence!" Mr. Baggot glared at his students. The whole lot were bound for Hell as it was—so why did he toil on their blighted behalfs? "William desires a question. He shall have one!" Slowly, he approached the apprentice. "A simple question, concerning his ancestors." He adjusted, then tightened, his grip on his staff.

"On a pole in Plymouth sits the head of the Indian Philip, the tawnies' blood-thirsting general. The Israelites too were assailed by godless tribes. When they fought against the Midianites, the heads of two of the enemy's princes were paraded as a sign of victory." Mr. Baggot paused, his eyes twinkling gaily. "I ask for but one of the princes' names."

His audience viewed him in disbelief. The Bible was as full of such names as the ocean was of fish.

"This question is not from our book," said William.

Mr. Baggot tucked *Spiritual Stepping-Stones for the Young* into a pocket and grinned. " 'Any question you choose' was your request." At last, the dark-skinned scholar had stumbled! The tithingman readied himself to leave a dent in his head to mark his triumph by.

"Not from our book," William continued, head low-

9

ered, "but from the book of Judges." Eyes closed, he reached back in his memory. "Chapter seven." Mr. Baggot's own pair opened wide in alarm.

" 'And they took two princes of the Midianites. . . .' " The apprentice raised his head. His eyelids lifted as if he were waking from a trance. "Oreb," he answered the tithingman.

Mr. Baggot's teeth scraped. His breathing became heavy. His skin tightened over his bony face as if drawn taut with a winch. Strangling the heavy staff in his hand, he leveled a murderous stare at William.

" 'Tis in my power to have you whipped at the public post," he stated softly, his body shaking from the effort of restraint. "Or to set you in the stocks or pillory. To have your ears lopped off, tongue bored with a burning awl, or your forehead branded. All I need do is find your foot a hair past the bounds of the laws of the town." He bent forward until their noses nearly touched. "And I want you to know that my eye is upon you. Like a spider's eye upon the fly." His voice had narrowed to a whisper. "And that one day soon— I'll snare you."

He straightened, turned, and strode out of the room. By ear, William followed his rapid progress through the rest of the house, decided against shouting the name of the other prince of the Midianites, and heard the front door slam.

All six children were set in motion by the sound: toward school, the outhouse, the pump, the spinning wheel.

"Keep your eyes skinned for him," counseled Sarah. William smiled. He entered the printing room, ubbed his hands against the cold, picked up his wooden composing stick, and began setting type as if nothing had happened. And what had? Mr. Baggot had asked him a question; he'd answered it, correctly. Was it sinful to remember well? His memory had always been strong, though in truth his focusing it on the Bible was closer to sport than worshipful study. He'd been born into the Narraganset tribe and disliked the Englishmen's heartless Jehovah. But he enjoyed demonstrating to Mr. Baggot that all Indians weren't witless, and took pleasure in turning the book's own words on the tithingman and others found to be flouting Christ's message of love and compassion.

Nimbly, he picked letters from the typecase, setting them side by side in his stick, then glanced at the title of the sermon he was setting: "He That Knows and Does Not His Master's Will Shall Be Beaten With Many Blows." He thought of Mr. Baggot's threatened punishments. Had a more brutal race of men than these Christians ever roamed the earth? How else but through their ruthlessness had he come to wake up in Boston this morning? He looked out at the snow and realized that was now exactly six years back to the December evening the English had attacked, slaying all before them, young and old, women as well as men, like their Lord's avenging angels. And avenging what? It was Philip and his Wampanoags the English were at war with. Merely out of the fear that the Narragansets

might join Philip's side, they'd been slaughtered b
the hundreds that night. Discovering that his finger
had stopped working, the apprentice roused himsel
strove to evict that topic from his thoughts, and reache
quickly for an "i," an "n," a "g," and then a perio

"How comes the sermon, William?" Mr. Currie,
heavy log under each arm, entered the room an
dropped the wood with a crash on the fire dozing i
the hearth, provoking a tirade of snapping and sparkin

"I've come to the torments in Hell awaiting unrul
servants," he replied. "Fetching hot coals with thei
bare hands. Polishing Satan's throne without end."

Mr. Currie sighed. "I suspect the author, Reveren
Peck, is vexed with his serving girl again." He prodde
the fire with an iron poker as if it were a balky cow
"Though 'tis certain you won't slave in Hades besid
her. I've never had an apprentice so quick-fingered wit
type."

William smiled inside. Like a frog's tongue, his righ
hand shot out and snapped up a capital "h," then a
"e," then a pair of "l"s. Mr. Currie, meanwhile, too
out a stone bowl and commenced mixing ink from
lampblack and oil.

"Are we sailing for Troy tonight?" asked the printer
By which means he'd inquired for the past severa
weeks whether William had studied three more page
of the *Iliad*, which the two of them and Sarah wer
reading together in Greek.

"Ready to raise anchor," came William's ritual reply
Mr. Currie nodded. Gwenne, the family's nineteen

ear-old serving girl, began sweeping out the weeks-ld, dirtied sand that protected the wooden floor.

"Have you spied the lump Mr. Baggot gave young Timothy?" she addressed the room.

Mr. Currie looked up and shook his head, fixed two ages of type in the press, and spread some ink on a marble slab.

"In faith, I ought to have swept the man out the loor with the other leavings," she declared. She wielded ler birch broom ferociously and gradually followed it out of the room. A minute later she returned, sowing landfuls of fresh white sand from a bucket. " 'Twould be joy to give *him* such a knock with his staff!"

"Soft now, Gwenne," cautioned Mrs. Currie. A smiling woman, whose fingernails were as likely to hold nk as her husband's, she led her young son James nto the room, lifted him onto a box so that his eyes ust cleared the top of a typecase, and continued her lesson on which letter was to be found in which compartment. A moment later, Amos, the printer's brawny ourneyman, strode inside, called out "Good day," and received five different-pitched echoes in reply. Warming his hands, he watched Mr. Currie tug on the press's long iron handle. "What are we pulling the Devil's tail for today?"

The press's timbers groaned, and inked type met dampened Dutch paper. "A tract on profane and promiscuous dancing." Mr. Currie carefully searched the page he'd printed for signs of damaged type. "Written by a deacon in Deerfield. He's against it."

William began setting the last page of his sermon, wherein lazy, insolent serving girls were pictured soot-blackened and sobbing, ceaselessly cleaning the myriad chimneys of Hell. Knowing where to find each letter without looking, he was able to keep watch on the world out the window and found himself smiling, given the text he was setting, at the sight of Mr. Hogwood and Malcolm, his manservant, trudging toward him up King Street. He watched them traverse a drift, the squat master's short legs nearly lost in the snow, while his long-legged servant traveled with ease. The pair crossed the road, stepping over the open sewer running down the middle, then skirted a trio of scavenging pigs. Mr. Hogwood's plump face and Malcolm's wedge-thin one passed like visions before William's window, following which the front bell tinkled, the apprentice left his place at the typecase, and found the two fully fleshed in the shop.

"A quire of Holland paper," Malcolm commanded importantly.

William departed the room to fetch it, leaving Mr. Hogwood to inspect the quill pens and his servant to put the time to profit by nodding, then grinning, then lifting his hat to a female passing by the front window.

William returned. Malcolm whirled from the window. "And a pair of quills!" he ordered, unaware that Mr. Hogwood had set two on the counter. The manservant paid for the purchases, placed them with the others in his basket, and ceremoniously opened the door for his master, trailing him down the street, as instructed, at a distance of two paces.

Left to his thoughts, Malcolm contemplated the physique of an approaching milkmaid, while Mr. Hogwood, barber and wigmaker, wondered at Mr. Currie's neglect of his appearance. The man was a printer, a position of respect, yet he paid no mind at all to his wig. It was shabby and hadn't been dressed in months, as was true as well of those to be found on his sons, apprentice, and journeyman. He surveyed the male heads in view, all of them properly wigged and hatted. What would become of the world if a man's attire no longer declared his station? The lion ruled over the fox, who was lord to the mouse; so it was as well among men. For which cause wigs were sold in a score of styles, each assigned to its own rank of wearers, that a magistrate might be known at once by his magnificent, perfumed cascade of curls, made from the finest human locks, while an oyster peddler's head might hold only a grimy scrap of horsehair. Though neither rich nor powerful, Mr. Hogwood, as upholder of this hierarchy, felt raised up within it and had adorned himself in the silk waistcoat, gold buttons, silver lace, and flowing wig of his betters, despite the fact that it was against the law to dress above one's station. Undeceived by his resplendent appearance, a mangy dog approached the wigmaker and sniffed at his calf with outrageous familiarity.

"Be off!" shouted Malcolm, moving up beside his master. He would turn twenty in a matter of weeks, old enough to be his own master, and had increasingly found the role of lagging lackey insufferable.

"Off now!" The dog dropped back; Malcolm stayed.

Mr. Hogwood cast him a look full of meaning. What use was there in parading your man if he humiliated you in public?

"Beware of yonder goats," said Malcolm solicitously, justifying his presence. He slowed his long legs to match his master's pace. "Mrs. Mott's shop's on the left, past the pump," he added, as if Mr. Hogwood didn't know. In further display of his services, he scouted a patch of treacherous footing, sent scurrying a succession of pigs, and defended his master from a foul-breathed fishwife before flinging open Mrs. Mott's door with a deference verging on mockery.

A savory braid of scent reached his nose, woven of fruitcakes, lemons, and wines. His eyes took in the equally pleasing sight of Mrs. Mott's comely shopgirl.

"Six of your sweetest oranges," said Malcolm. He grinned, his teeth glinting like winter stars, and received a modest smile from the girl. Finding his master scrutinizing the rums and brandies, he approached her more closely. "Plus a half pound of raisins," he whispered, then winked. The girl nodded knowingly. Malcolm took stock of her body's many advantages while she stooped for the one item and ascended a short stepladder for the other. Paying for both, he promised to return the favor at a future date, winked, and nearly yanked the door off its hinges in honor of his master's exit.

"The cost?" asked the wigmaker.

"One shilling tenpence," Malcolm answered truthfully. He'd found that Mr. Hogwood kept track of the

16

money entrusted to him for purchases, and that each missing penny had to be accounted for.

His master stopped short. "For a mere six oranges?" He held down his hat against a thieving gust of wind.

"The girl said they're extremely choice," explained Malcolm. "Brought all the way from Spain." The wigmaker snorted. He moved on again, as did Malcolm, at his side. "And 'tis sure you want the choicest to be found. Considering who's to receive them."

Mr. Hogwood angrily flapped his hand, motioning Malcolm back two paces, from the safety of which position the servant commenced to feast on the raisins in his pocket.

Following the path worn through the snow, Mr. Hogwood mused on Malcolm's words. He was right—this was no time to think of expense. Madam Phipp, after all, was accustomed to fine foods. In winter she probably dined every day upon sweet-smelling fruits from the earth's four corners, rather than on beets from the root cellar, like most. Nevertheless, he imagined her gobbling up all six oranges at a sitting, enchanted by their taste and aroma, gratefully murmuring his name. It would be his first proper courtship gift. Malcolm, who appeared quite learned in such things, had particularly recommended oranges. Mr. Hogwood hoped his advice was sound. Widows, he knew, didn't stay widows long. Her home had likely been swarmed by men at the news of her wealthy husband's demise. As if God had meant Mr. Hogwood to make the most of this chance for social advancement, He'd plucked Mrs.

17

Hogwood off the earth the next week. And though he'd long sneered at his wife's common forebears, the wigmaker had been pleased by the sum, inherited from her grandfather, that had come to him upon her death—which money he'd invested in the fine clothes on his frame and the servant at his stern.

" 'Tis Madam Phipp's bakeshop on the left," declared Malcolm, discreetly advancing to his master's side.

Mr. Hogwood glared at him and wondered how it was that he seemed to know everything. A passing woman flashed Malcolm a smile. And every*one*, the wigmaker added. Envious of the scamp's handsome features, he shooed him to the rear, then saw Mr. Baggot approaching and haughtily raised his head. "Devilish bushes of vanity" was the tithingman's stock pronouncement on wigs. He was one of a weakening wig-hating faction, several of whom over the past months had furtively made their way to Mr. Hogwood's to have their heads shaved, measured, and re-covered. He glanced at Mr. Baggot's own hair as they passed—grimy, flame red, pathetically sparse—and smirked at the ludicrous sight. Poor man!

"Madam Phipp has her shoes repaired here," spoke up Malcolm, slipping forward yet again.

Mr. Hogwood scowled at his manservant.

"Of course," he went on, "her new shoes come from England. Purchased by her sister-in-law in London." He led his master around a mound of dung, brushed some snow from his beaver hat, and kept his place by bubbling forth more news of Madam Phipp up Water

18

street, down Cornhill, past the Town House, and back to their shop at the head of King Street.

Malcolm majestically opened the door, and Mr. Hogwood's journeymen and apprentices instantly jerked to life like string puppets, blowing away crumbs, leaping from naps, and setting furiously to work with needle, curling iron, and comb.

"Any tidings of import?" the wigmaker asked.

All but one shook their heads "no," as if they were too immersed in their tasks to spare the use of their tongues.

"Charity snared another mouse," piped up Dan, Mr. Hogwood's young nephew and newest apprentice. Just come to Boston the day before, knowing nothing of the wigmaking trade, he'd been given house chores and immediately had dropped a log on his uncle's toe. Frantic to impress his snarling master, he'd taken upon himself to rid the ceilings of cobwebs in his absence this morning, managing to fall but twice and to break no more than six mugs and one chair. Hoping to please further, he now pointed out the latest mouse's head left on the floor by the shop's industrious cat.

"At least someone here earns his keep," snapped Mr. Hogwood. He signaled Malcolm to remove his cloak. "Have you sluggards left it on the floor all morning?"

Dan darted forward and snatched it up. "Where would you have me put it, Uncle?"

"Anywhere, thickwit!" thundered Mr. Hogwood. "Just take it away ere a customer comes!"

19

His nephew vanished with it in his hands, while the wigmaker wondered how such a wormy fruit had appeared on the family tree. Six years he'd have to endure the boy! Trying to calm himself, he approached the featureless wooden head that held a wig belonging to Madam Phipp's footman, returned to the shop for a routine dressing. Mr. Hogwood picked up a tortoise-shell comb. Though its wearer was male, the wig's brown hair had come from a woman, females' hair having been found to be stronger than men's. Rounding curls, shaping, straightening, his fingers moved up one row and down another, as if laboring in a garden of hair. Gradually, his thick lips formed a smile. He began to hum and felt his cares retreat, replaced by the pleasing fancy that he was running his hands through the ravishing chestnut locks of Madam Phipp herself.

A gentleman entered the shop to be shaved, followed by another to have a tooth pulled. A burly hair merchant paid a call and filled the wigmaker's order for more flaxen, black, and gray hair from England. Finishing with the footman's wig, Mr. Hogwood took one of the sheets of paper bought at the printer's shop that morning and snipped it into quarters with his scissors. He folded one of the quarters in half, dipped a pen in ink, and wrote "With the Special Compliments of Samuel Hogwood, Wigmaker, King Street, Boston." Opening the door to a wig box, he draped the wig over the stand inside, then added the card, something he did only with wigs from Madam Phipp's household, to no perceptible effect so far. Malcolm then served him the cook's noon meal of boiled parsnips, codfish cakes, and apple slump, washed down with the beer it was a manservant's duty to brew in the cellar. Having yet to master this craft's finer points, along with several of its major principles, Malcolm noted Mr. Hogwood's grimace upon his first swig of the potent concoction, and his loss of concentration on his food after six or seven more. Belching, the wigmaker rose from the table, squinted, searched his yeast-clouded wits, and just succeeded in remembering, on his way upstairs for an unaccustomed nap, to tell his manservant to deliver the wig and oranges to Madam Phipp that afternoon.

"Yes, sir," answered Malcolm. Abhorring waste, and cold cod, he quickly finished his master's meal while the food was still warm. After eating the same fare again with the other members of the household, he divided the oranges among his pockets, took up the wig box by its handle, and set off.

Gaily, Malcolm whistled a tune. When alone on errands he felt gloriously free, at no one's beck and call but his own. Then again, he reflected, picking up an orange, this outing was another proof of his slavery—for why else had Mr. Hogwood sent him but to impress Madam Phipp with the fact that he now had a servant to tramp the streets in his place? The wig box in one hand, he held the orange to his mouth with the other, peeled it with his teeth, and cast the skin to a pig. His mood gone sour, he sweetened his mouth with the heavenly juice and began to feel better. For months he'd been craving the taste of an orange, and he thanked his suggestive master for satisfying his desire.

He stopped before a dressmaker's window. Appraising his reflection in detail, he adjusted his wig, straightened his hat, inspected his smile, cleaned out both nostrils, ignored the rude gestures of the woman within, and continued two doors down to a cookshop. There he traded an orange to the owner's alluring daughter for a glass of ale, a squeeze of her hand, and a smuggled leg of lamb. Explaining that he had an errand to accomplish, he strode off in the direction of Boston Neck, made his way to a merchant's rear door, and was asked in by a serving girl of his acquaintance. Over three glasses of pilfered wine, the two warmed themselves at the hearth and traded gossip of their respective masters. Before leaving, due to the press of his duties, Malcolm presented the girl with an orange, described its journey from Spain and great cost, and extracted two kisses in recompense. He traveled on and happened to meet in the street a stony-faced shopgirl he knew. Assuring her that she alone owned his heart, he found her doubtful, saw that the orange he'd planned to bestow would most likely be squandered, ate it himself, and at last reached Madam Phipp's.

The house was of brick, many-gabled and grand. He glimpsed a black servant unhitching Madam Phipp's gleaming carriage from her matched team of horses. He ascended the steps and rapped loudly with the knocker. African slaves, a coach house for her carriage, a chandelier hanging over his head . . . Malcolm's calculation of the woman's worth was interrupted by the opening of the door.

"Yes?"

He grinned at the serving girl before him, brown-haired and big-eyed and unknown to him. "Malcolm Poole at your service," he stated. He inventoried her sleek body with a glance.

Knowingly, the girl eyed the wig box. "At my service, and someone else's, I warrant."

The manservant parried this thrust with a smile. " 'Tis true that I recently engaged myself to Mr. Hogwood, a wigmaker," he conceded. This was his euphemism for the fact that his master had paid for his passage from England and was due five long years of Malcolm's labor in return, all but nine weeks of which he still owed. "That service, of course, pertains solely to the body," Malcolm elaborated. "My service to you pertains to the soul. That soft-voiced master within your breast, for whom I—"

His speech was cut short by the girl's grabbing the wig box and slamming the heavy door on his quickly inserted boot.

"Whom 'twould be utter rapture to serve," he continued through the narrow opening. "Who bellows not for more stew or a hotter fire or to have his boots tugged off. But who asks of her servant only love." His hands reached quickly into a pocket. "As a sign of my allegiance, I'd like to present you with a small gift." He considered giving her both remaining oranges, then remembered that it was in his own interests to keep Mr. Hogwood's courtship alive, that the flow of gifts, so useful, might continue. Feeling one fruit and then the other, he drew out the larger, handed it through, and heard it fall on the floor.

"My master also wished me to leave a token of his

regard for your mistress." Though the girl was thin, so was his boot leather, and Malcolm found her pressing with such force that he had to deftly substitute his other foot in the door. Digging out of his waistcoat pocket the last, smallest, and hardest of the oranges, Malcolm heard the serving girl strain, feared he'd soon be crippled, and tried to deliver the fruit while withdrawing his foot—with the unfortunate result that Madam Phipp's gift was crushed in her doorway, splitting its skin, spurting forth juice, and spitting its seeds in all directions, two of which struck Malcolm on the nose before he fled down the front steps in retreat.

The girl, he concluded while hobbling home, was not entirely in his grasp. Yet.

T W O

BY HALF PAST FIVE that afternoon the stars shone over Boston. By six o'clock shops were shut tight for the night. By seven thirty a great many of their owners had digested their dinners, read from their Bibles, and heated their sheets with the warming pan. In place of the sun, the light atop Beacon Hill now watched over town and harbor with its unblinking, oil-burning eye. Day birds dreamed. Owls awakened. And Boston's nocturnal citizens emerged.

Night watchmen relieved the town's nine constables. In the Common, three pairs of courters, hearts sizzling and noses frozen, strode briskly through the snow. A runaway eyeglass maker's apprentice, his pockets bulging with rolls, dashed up Pond Street, then headed toward the town gate. While in front of the Mermaid Tavern, on King Street, Mr. Benjamin Henry Tillstone, known as Tut, unfolded the wooden stand for his telescope.

"Penny a peep!" he informed the world at large, a world uninhabited at the moment except by himself and his dog curled nearby. A bustling man, small and lean as his whippet, he sunk the stand's legs into the snow, attached the three-foot-long telescope, and inspected its swivel. "Penny a peep!" Working by the light from the Mermaid's window, he produced this call, froglike, three more times in the course of cleaning the eyepiece with a cloth, busily polishing the brass barrel, and then training it on a light in the east. "Gaze through the glass at the planet Saturn!"

Two men left the tavern, one of whom stated his fear that should he look through the contrivance he'd at once find himself transported to the stars. The other, scoffing at such ignorance, paid his penny, viewed Saturn's rings, and stormed away declaring the sight had been painted inside the instrument.

"Penny a peep!" Tut patted his dog, white as the snow on which she lay. Gently, he examined her splinted front leg. "Behold the marvels of God's firmament!"

Four men in succession loomed out of the darkness of the unlit street, each passing Tut by. The telescope exhibitor sighed. Just as his name had suffered a shortening during his stint in the British Navy, so his forunes had recently narrowed. Prone to put the best ace on things, he pulled out the night's first coin, miled, and gazed up at the sky from which it had come. The heavens were now his fruitful fields, the telescope his plowshare and sickle. Clouds were his locusts, and winter his summer, when the nights were long and the stars bright as diamonds. Blowing upon his ungloved fingers, he told himself that the cold months were a blessing. Especially since his career demonstrating sleights of hand with cards and dice had been abruptly brought to a close three weeks back, the result of a tithingman's complaint that had led him to be ordered by a judge to find a more praiseworthy line of work. Turning to his dog's talent for tricks, he'd passed his hat at cookshops and groggeries while narrating, in a reverent tone, the canine's tributes to the glory of God's animal creations. This living had quickly ended with the dog's falling from a pyramid of five chairs, snapping a leg and leaving her master as well without any means of support but the much-dented telescope before him.

"Penny a peep!" he addressed a pair of passersby, to no avail. He hugged himself against the cold, his ragged doublet and breeches offering the winter air a wide choice of entrances. Trying to breathe life into his fingers, he glimpsed the Mermaid's hearth through the window and longed to be earning his living indoors. Then again, he begged to differ with himself, his was a pleasant trade. Plenty of time to think your own thoughts, and none of the alehouses' uproar and stale air. He looked up at Orion rising in the east and smiled as at the approach of a friend. Then he spied three men trudging up the street and swiveled the telescope to the north.

"I've Andromeda in the glass for your pleasure! Chained to a rock to be eaten by the sea monster! Saved by Perseus riding his flying horse. All for the price of a penny!" The men, jabbering in a foreign tongue, warily avoided Tut, leaving him staring down at his dog. But for you, he brooded, we could both be warm as coals. And yet, he pointed out in reply, you learned quite a lot with the telescope. Taking the advice of the nautical instrument maker from whom he'd bought it third-hand, he'd purchased a book on the constellations and had increased his business a good deal by describing the shocking goings-on overhead, which deeds a certain percentage of his patrons expected to actually witness through the glass.

Two rum-sodden sailors staggered out of the Mermaid.

"Princess Andromeda, comely as a May queen, here in the glass!" beckoned Tut.

The first one succeeded in stopping his legs. "Bonny wench, is she?" he slurred with some interest.

"Ask her if her pa's at home," barked the other, bumping blindly into his companion. "Don't want any bother from him, do we now?"

Tut aimed the pair down the street and sighed. How would he pay for his lodging at this rate? The telescope, he'd been promised by its seller, would feed and clothe him the rest of his days. He considered the location he'd chosen. There was no better thoroughfare than King Street. And the Mermaid was a popular spot. Perhaps if he planted a torch in the snow, by way of attracting—

"Algol," said a voice.

Tut gave a start, as if the night itself had spoken, whirled around, and found himself facing a man instead.

"Algol," he repeated. "The demon star."

"Yes, sir," sputtered Tut. "Straightaway, sir." He felt an additional chill climb his spine. "If you're certain 'tis the one you wish."

Gravely, the man nodded in reply. Tut aimed the telescope almost straight up, rummaged among the stars and planets, then drew back his head. "There you are." He smiled, yet felt cheerless within, and watched uneasily as his patron, towering over Tut by two heads, slowly stooped and put his eye to the glass.

"Saturn's bright as a button tonight," chirped Tut. "Would you care for a gawk at that too?"

His customer offered no reply. Nervously, Tut cleared his throat and eyed the man's long, coffin-shaped face. It was not the first time he'd looked through the telescope. Two weeks back, when Tut had first set up the instrument near the Town Dock, the man had materialized out of the night. Later, when he'd tried out a spot near Belcher's wharf, he'd approached Tut again. He always paid well, far more than Tut's price, as if money mattered little to him.

And yet, his clothes were as tattered as Tut's own. And he always asked to view this same star, despite its frightening associations. . . .

" 'Tis fiendish cold tonight," Tut piped up, then wondered if his patron might be a tithingman. "As the Lord meant winter to be," he added.

Apparently not in reply to Tut, the man muttered the words "I see you." His teeth were clenched. His hands trembled slightly. "I'm looking upon your face," he hissed. His voice was no longer private, but public. "Do you hear? Staring into your awful eye!"

Tut's dog raised its ears. Breathing heavily, the man squinted through the eyepiece, then pulled back his head in disgust, straightened up, and finding that Tut had retreated toward the Mermaid, dropped a pair of gold coins on the tramped-down snow at his feet and continued up King Street.

Shuffling slowly through the crusted snow, he cursed the star that had failed him again, glimpsed a man with a lantern approaching, and decided against ducking down an alley. It was now three months back to the September morning his daughter had died of smallpox, and to the night he'd begun taking aimless walks. As he was known by day as a hardworking man—his shop sign declared him to be Joseph Speke, Furniture Maker and Carver of Sign Boards, Mantelpieces, &c.—he'd at first hoped to hide his time-wasteful wanderings, concocting elaborate excuses for his wife and for anyone met in the streets. Lately, however, he'd ceased to bother. He exchanged raised hats with the passerby.

Sturdy arms crossed beneath his frayed cape, Mr. Speke burrowed ahead through the blackness. He turned down a narrow lane, then turned again, stopped, wondered where he was, then found he was standing nearby the sundial in front of his brother's apothecary shop. He approached the stone column and felt the brass dial. He ran his fingers over the roman numerals, then over the inscription whose words he couldn't make out but knew from memory: "The Hour Is At Hand."

Mr. Speke walked on, eyed the almost-full moon, and meditated on the sundial's motto. Days had shortened to mere interludes between nights. The gloating moon was now master of the sky, the frail winter sun her vassal. No green thing grew. No insect sang. The once-soft earth was stiff beneath the snow. The hour was indeed at hand. The world was dying. Judgment was near. A thought the wood-carver found comforting.

He strolled to the end of a wharf and stood, listening to the conversation of the waters. Before his daughter had died, he reflected, he'd never have been found at this spot, at this hour. Nor would he have stared through a telescope at Algol, the star denoting the face of Medusa, the snake-headed face reputed to turn all who looked upon it to stone. But since then his heart had slowly frozen, like a pond icing from the edges inward. He'd begun to long for his own demise, to yearn for his naked soul to be judged. A soul burdened by a deed accounted most commendable by all. By all, that is, but Mr. Speke himself.

31

The carver lifted his eyes to the sky. Two shooting stars dropped from the heavens, sowing themselves among the ocean's furrows. He thought of his Dora, a sweet-voiced child of three, incomparably precious to him, her face scarlet and streaming with sweat. He inhaled deeply, and for the thousandth time since she'd died, recalled another December, back during his service in the Indian war, and endured the remembrance of another girl—running, a wooden ladle in her hand, a girl whose face he hadn't seen but whose endless shrieking tormented him whenever he closed his eyes to sleep, the source of his night meanderings.

He turned and started back up the wharf, passing the warehouse of Mr. Epp, who'd engaged him to carve a figurehead for his new brig, soon to set sail. The man had badgered him about it again this morning, the third time in a week. Despite which, as in matters of clothing and money, Mr. Speke had found himself hard put to care. He'd always sculpted the figures from live models, and of late he'd been unable to disengage himself from the world of the dead.

"You there!"

Mr. Speke peered into the darkness.

" 'Tis past curfew!" bellowed the speaker. "What's your business?"

A lantern's beam advanced down the wharf, jerking back and forth and followed by the large, beet-shaped bulk of Absalom Trulliber, night watchman. Breathing noisily, he stopped a foot before the wood-carver and examined his catch from the top down with his light.

"Taking the air, to help me sleep," said Mr. Speke. "I never heard the curfew bell."

Mr. Trulliber shone his lantern on the carver's feet, as if he might possibly find hoofs or flippers there instead. Apparently satisfied, he stepped back.

"Up with your jib and be off then," he ordered. "Take the air in your *bedchamber*, like the others." His voice was scornful. With a pitying smirk, he watched as the man ambled on and finally disappeared from view.

Sleepers! The watchman snorted his contempt for that sorry class of humanity. The moment the sun slipped out of sight they rushed toward their mattresses, snoring away the hours, knowing nothing of night. While Mr. Trulliber and his colleagues, members of a small and superior caste, walked the silent streets until dawn, fleshly replicas of the all-seeing and ever-vigilant Lord.

He headed back up the wharf, glancing haughtily at the moon. He didn't need its help in lighting his way. Or his lantern's, he often bragged. He claimed he could read the Bible by the light of a single star, and that his mole's eyes found midnight as bright as noon. Trudging steadily through the blackness, he searched with those eyes for any sign of fire, cocked his ear for fiddling or singing, then cut short the dreams of dozens of sleepers with his stentorian calling out of the hour— "Ten o'clock!"—and his self-contradicting description of the night, "And all quiet!"

Keeping close to the water, he sighted the shipyard where he wielded mallet and plane by day and napped

33

briefly each noontime. Farther on, he brought to a halt a tipsy, Swedish-speaking seaman and informed him in incomprehensible English that all persons were to be in by nine o'clock. So that, he added privately, the exalted corps of watchmen might be undisturbed in their serene, planetlike circuits through the sleeping town.

Two streets away, another regular traveler through the Boston night, one unknown to Mr. Trulliber, crept out of a door, fastened his cloak at the throat, took stock of the night, and set off. Having studied the watchmen's orbits closely and seen Mr. Trulliber pass a minute earlier, he started cautiously up King Street, then headed toward Mill Cove.

The sky above him shimmered with lights like some vast illuminated city. The earthly town below was black but for the beacon gleaming on his left, close enough to cast his shadow. He studied this silhouette while he walked, then noticed that the moon had given him another, slanting in a different direction. He stopped and eyed the doubled being before him. No limner, he mused, could have drawn him more faithfully. He had known two worlds, had lived two lives, had even been called by two different names: Weetasket, bestowed by his father at birth, and William, the name he'd worn in his second life, chosen by his second father, the printer Mr. Currie.

He moved stealthily down Sudbury Street, thinking of the Curries at home in their beds. They were all sound sleepers, except the infant Rose. It had always

34

een easy to slip out undetected. What a shock it would ome to them, and to so many others, to know where e was just then. He shuddered at the thought. He ust never be caught! They'd think him another deeitful Indian. How could he face Mr. Currie again? t supper he'd felt as gleeful as the others, planning ne coming Saturnalia—imagining the feast, hatching nischiefs, guessing who'd reign as the King or Queen. fterward, he and Sarah and Mr. Currie had together ored over three more pages of the *Iliad* in its original ongue, taking them to the fleet's landing at Troy. He oved reading Homer and deciphering Greek. He loved Ir. Currie and his family, into which he'd been welomed like another son. Six sunny years he'd lived mong them. But though his memories of the eight ears before had begun fading, like footprints in falling now, he hadn't forgotten his first family's faces. hey'd loved him as well. Which thought now and hen interrupted his typesetting or reading, and which ow drove his legs through the empty streets.

He glimpsed Mill Cove ahead, reached into a pocket, nd pulled out a small bone flute. Cautiously, he lanced about. Then he put the flute to his lips and egan playing softly, capping and uncovering its holes, eleasing a restful tune into the night. Its scale and hythm were foreign to the psalms and ballads heard n Boston. It wandered like a rivulet, patient, peaceful, vhile William viewed the windows he passed.

He turned left down an alley, then right, his path vinding through the town like a night-growing vine.

The song he was playing had been learned from his father, one of the three from his past that he'd managed to keep alive in his memory. The flute from which it uncurled had been made by his grandfather from the wing bone of a heron. It was the one object he possessed from his old life, and its sound always led him back to the sweet aroma of his father's stone pipe, the taste of parched cornmeal and ripe cranberries, the feel of the deerskin on which he'd slept. He was good at memorizing, he realized, because he'd more to remember than most people. His first world had been swept away in a day. To preserve that world, if only in his mind, had seemed to him, when he'd first reached Boston, a duty owed to the dead. Zealously filling his memory since with Latin quotations and Greek verb tenses, the Kings of Israel and the craft of printing, he'd found it a duty increasingly difficult to carry out.

He strode up a new street and probed a lit window. He thought back to summer days spent in scaring off crows with his brothers, searching for them from the watchhouses built among the fields of corn. Glancing about him while he played, he now watched for something else entirely: for the face of a boy who would know the flute's music, whose eyes would spring open and who'd dash to the window. A boy who'd also played a bone flute—Cancasset, his own twin brother.

A dog began barking at him, then another. Quickly he bribed them with breadcrusts from his pocket, then spied a moving light in the distance. A watchman heading left. William stopped. He wondered if he'd been playing too loudly. And at once he recalled an added danger: Mr. Baggot. A watchman might only ask his business; the tithingman would strive to see him whipped until his blood puddled on the ground.

He turned a corner and walked toward the west, softening his music slightly. His flute had rarely brought unwanted notice. Each time he'd easily escaped, having had plenty of practice at avoiding capture. When the English had attacked the Narragansets, he and Cancasset had been among the first to flee the island village. They'd dashed across the Great Swamp, frozen solid, had dug up a cache of buried food, and had made a shelter from fallen branches. His brother had even succeeded in stealing a musket from a sleeping soldier. For a week they'd evaded the English, then been surprised returning to their camp and caught. They'd been marched to Plymouth, then separated. William had continued on with a score of fellow prisoners to Boston, where they were assigned as servants to those who wished them and where he'd been apprenticed to Mr. Currie. It was from others that he'd learned that his father had fallen early in the battle; that his mother and sisters had perished when the soldiers had set fire to the village; that one brother had been shipped to the sugar plantations of the West Indies as a slave, while another had escaped westward into the country of the Niantics. He'd several times glimpsed his oldest brother, swaying for days from the gallows on the Common, hanged for taking up arms against the English. But no one knew what had become of Cancasset.

A wolf bayed off in the distance. William knew it was late and pointed his toes toward Mr. Currie's. After six years of intermittent searching, he was scarcely disappointed by his lack of success. He held little hope that he would find his brother. Of necessity, he'd learned to live without him. An impossible feat, he'd felt at first. He now thought about him far less than he once had. Still, he couldn't help wondering if he might perchance be in Boston, if he were sleeping in a bed tonight or on deerskin, whether he was being treated kindly or cruelly. And whether he and the rest of his clan would be proud of William's shining success in the world of the English—or scornful. Would they curse him for joining the enemy? Taunt him with being as English as King Charles? If nothing else, he hoped that his hopeless searches would at least quiet his conscience and show those remembered faces that he hadn't entirely forgotten them.

An owl swooped past William's head. Hardly aware, wrapped in his thoughts, he marched ahead down Middle Street. So absorbed that he failed to notice the outline of a scrawny young man, humming and wearing a low-brimmed hat, who scuttled deeper into the darkness like a crab and with great interest watched the apprentice pass an eyeglass maker's shop, slip his flute into a pocket, blow on his hands, and turn toward King Street.

THREE

T RAVELING BY DAYLIGHT, several mornings later, William made his way down crowded Queen Street, out on a round of errands. The December air might have been borrowed from May. Snow was softening in the streets and melting furiously from roofs, as if winter had given up its siege of the city. Birds chattered gaily in the treetops. The apprentice, however, felt none of their cheer. Stopping at an alley, he plucked the note from his pocket and peered at the words one more time.

> Brother,
> Join others of our kind in driving

the villainous English from the land.
Cautantowwit demands it. Noon,
The Pearl Tavern, Flint's Alley

He studied the unfamiliar handwriting, then buried
the paper in his waistcoat and strode on. Could it be,
he wondered, that Cancasset had found *him*, rather
than the other way around? He'd heard at Mr. Currie's
that another Narraganset servant had recently arrived,
lodging somewhere in the North End. Or was "brother"
merely a figure of speech? Either way, it was prohibited
for servants or apprentices to visit taverns. And to do
so to plan a war on the English! The thumbscrews,
stocks, and gallows combined would scarcely satisfy
the magistrates' wrath.

He passed the First Church, neared the Town House,
and saw a group gathered about the whipping post.
Though not of a mind to stand and watch, he found
his head turning that way as he walked and spied,
through the crowd, several slivers of the scene: flecks
of blood on a swan-white back, the flogger's groan as
he arched his spine so as to bring down his whip to
full advantage, the report that the woman tied to the
post had been heard maligning the Governor. William's
heart sped wildly at this news. Why was he carrying
the note around with him? He ought to have flung it
into the fire! His gaze on the ground, fearful his secret
could be read in his eyes, he swore he would do exactly
that the instant he reached home.

He entered a pungent shop on his right and purchased

tobacco for Mr. Currie's pipe. Continuing on, he added to his basket a parcel of pins ordered from England, delivered to their author twelve just-printed pamphlets extracting God's message from the fall's smallpox scourge, then quickly filled that hole with nettle tops, nutmegs, and cloves for the printer's wife.

He commenced the trek back toward Mr. Currie's, his mind, unlike his feet, aimed all morning in one direction: the note. Even though it was sealed with wax and addressed to William, hadn't its writer been foolish to leave it out in plain sight, slipped underneath the shop's front door? Or had it been written by someone who'd carefully studied the daily routine of the house? Someone who knew that William rose first, to light the fires, and would find it? Its author was surely a Narraganset to have claimed that Cautantowwit, the creator, had ordered the overthrow of the English. But what sort of tavern would be safe for such a meeting? Was its owner a Frenchman, keen to kindle an Indian rising against his country's foe?

A flock of questions flitting about his head, William marched along the harbor. He avoided a cart and dodged a string of casks being rolled through the slushy street. Then he halted, eyes wide. Flint's Alley was on his right.

He stood still as a scarecrow, amazed at where he was. Apprehensively, he scanned the alley. It was narrow and dim, its snow standing deep. Halfway down he glimpsed a signboard, fanged with icicles and featuring in its center a moonlike, painted pearl.

A passing broom seller bumped off William's hat. A slave merchant tugging two black children wearing chains and very little else barked at the apprentice to move aside. Not wanting to attract any further notice, he abruptly turned up the alley as if he'd been headed that way all along. The very lane, he castigated himself, that he'd vowed to avoid!

He neared the tavern, heard voices, smelled food. He told himself he would just stride by it. He hadn't come for the meeting, after all—he'd no notion of the hour. And as for rooting the English out of the country, the task was impossible. Even if it weren't, would he wish to see the Curries murdered, their house in flames? He would just walk past, out of curiosity. But as he approached and glanced at the door, he found his steps slowed by the thought that Cancasset himself might be on the other side. He felt light-headed, flooded with hope. How could he pass up a chance to meet the twin brother he'd spent six years searching for? Or if not him, perhaps another Narraganset who knew where he was.

William's feet stopped. He eyed the door latch. Half disbelieving, he watched his right hand reach out for it, felt the iron in his fingers—then froze. The noon bell was ringing! He'd be thought a member of the conspiracy, borne out by the hour given on the note! And at once he saw not a door before him but a gallows, heard the tolling of the bell and recalled his older brother swinging back and forth from his rope like a pendulum.

42

As if it were molten, he dropped the latch. He stepped back, nearly slipped, then burst into a run, clutching his basket to his chest and bounding through the snow like a deer—to the great disappointment of Mr. Baggot within, the note's author, who saw him fly past the window.

On William sped, not stopping until Flint's Alley was far behind him. Passing a blacksmith's shed, he entered, tossed the note into the forge, and watched the flames fight over the morsel. He scurried on and reached the printer's. Opening the door to the comforting scents of ink, paper, and Mrs. Currie's cooking, he closed his eyes, immensely grateful to be home and relieved he'd not entered The Pearl.

The door's brass bell jingled. "You there! Printer's devil!"

The words cut short William's giving of thanks.

"Trouble and plague! Attend me, boy!"

He knew the sharp-clawed voice at once. Girding himself, he turned as expected toward the ancient Mr. Rudd.

"I wish twenty handbills! In good speed, do you hear? Ere the scoundrel dashes clear to Virginia!" Stiff-backed and withered as a dried smelt, the eyeglass maker glared at William.

"And which scoundrel might this be?" he asked, as if he didn't know full well.

"My latest 'prentice!" raged Mr. Rudd. He grasped the awl that hung from his neck by a long leather cord and jabbed at the air. "He'll feel the devil's pitch-

fork, he will. Along with the rest of the race of ser
vants!"

His jagged chin advanced upon William. "Wha
shameless sins could have brought down upon us such
a plague of saucy, malingering scamps?" He fixed upon
William an accusing gaze, multiplied by the ten pairs
of hostile-eyed pewter buttons running down his coat

"But before you slink off in the night like the rest
see that you put this in type." He unfolded a sheet of
paper and thrust it at William, who focused his eyes
on the text.

Runaway Sought. Apprentice to Eyeglass Maker.
Fifteen Years in Age, of middling Stature,
Face well pitted from the Pox. Wears his own
Hair, brown and most unruly, befitting his
Character. Comes to the name of Solomon Moody
when he has a Mind to. Fled the 13th Night
of December. Any Person who brings him to the
Shop of Mr. Rudd, Middle Street, Boston
shall receive 40 Shillings for his Pains.

"Scarce two months and a half the rogue stayed!"
cried Mr. Rudd. "Trouble and plague!"

William, who'd set such handbills for him before,
was hardly surprised by this fact. The man was notori-
ous for being stingy with food and overgenerous with
his three-corded whip.

"Further, the knave took a dozen rolls with him!
A blunt-brained apprentice at grinding glass, but a master at shirking and a journeyman thief!" The eyeglass
maker's bony hands fisted. "But he'll smart for it,

tawny. Mark me, he will! He'll learn what it means to sign himself into the service of Mr. Uriah Rudd!"

Eyes bright with vengeance, he whirled about, tugged upon his black wig where it failed to fully cover his own white hair, cursed the nameless apprentice who was likely to blame for the error, and stalked away. Leaving a ravenous William to join the rest of the family for a plate of fried eels and a bowl of hotchpotch stew.

"Did I detect the angel-voiced Mr. Rudd?" asked the printer above the slurping and clatter of eleven mouths being fed.

"In faith," replied William. "The angel of death, hunting his latest apprentice. The boy's fled."

"Displays good sense in the lad," said Mrs. Currie.

" 'Tis said the vulture skims his milk at both ends," the journeyman Amos announced, and guffawed to the hearth and back for more stew.

Mr. Currie emptied his tankard of ale. "Ungrateful gluttons!" His impish eyes glittered. "Without the man's endless stream of handbills, shouldn't we starve in a fortnight ourselves?"

"The fallacy of exaggeration," Sarah protested at once. "Mr. Lee's now instructing me in logic," she added, winning a wink and a "Well spoken" from her father.

The serving girl Gwenne fetched two mince pies. "How I should love to set my eyes on a Saturnalia at Mr. Rudd's and see *him* serve his servants for a day! Flying about the house at their bidding! Kicked for his pains, then flogged for good measure!"

Mrs. Currie inserted a spoonful of broth into the

mouth of the baby Rose. "I believe you fright me, Gwenne, more than he does."

"And as a Saturnalia *shall* be held here," said her husband, "with my rank the bottommost, I beg you, no talk of kicks and whips!" A plea for mercy that brought from his children a dozen new whispered escapades to be executed on the approaching day. Retreating from the table in mock terror, Mr. Currie returned to his printing press, followed soon after by William, who'd no sooner picked up his composing stick than the shop's bell bade him set it down.

He entered the sun-filled front room. "Yes, sir."

This offer of service received no reply from Mr. Hogwood, eyeing the shop's stock of books, or Malcolm, equally intent on a female fruitseller passing the window. Reluctant to let her slip out of his sight, the manservant squinted, then bent to the left, banging his head on the glass and nearly punching two panes into the street, glanced about, and spied William with surprise. "Mr. Hogwood wishes to purchase a book!" he declared with all the dignity of his office.

William turned his eyes on the wigmaker, who brought Malcolm to his side with a snap of his fingers. "What think you of this?" he asked under his breath, not wishing such discussion overheard. In his hand was a copy of Munk's *Christian Marriage*.

The manservant meditated on the choice, then stooped to reach his short master's ear. "Too bold, I fear," he whispered in answer. "She may startle like a doe."

Mr. Hogwood scowled impatiently. To court was to enter a perilous wilderness of cliffs and avalanches, where a single misstep might mean one's end. He shoved the book back on the shelf, then pulled out a handsomely bound Latin grammar.

"We must also be wary of sending her to sleep," Malcolm counseled sagely.

Incensed at his use of "we," the wigmaker wrathfully motioned the upstart away. Madam Phipp would brook no such familiarity from her servants and neither would he. He leafed through the pages of an almanac. He considered an herbal. Then again, he reflected, although he admired his beloved's firmness with inferiors, *she* wasn't charged with choosing courtship gifts. He snapped his fingers for Malcolm once more.

"What say you to Wigglesworth's *Day of Doom*?"

The manservant cogitated deeply. "I believe we may wish to avoid," he whispered, "any link in her mind between marriage to you and the torments of the damned."

Mr. Hogwood, desperate, ignored Malcolm's "we." "Hang the business! You select it!"

Speedily, Malcolm scanned the shelves. He drew out a collection of sermons by Dr. Mather, inspected the contents, the binding, the paper, then offered it to his master. " 'Twill speak to her of your high-minded nature, and your tender concern for her soul."

Mr. Hogwood, unaware until then that his concern reached beyond her wealth and rank, waved the book away. "Very well!"

47

At these words, William ceased his inventory of the room's inkhorns and quills.

"Mr. Hogwood wishes this volume!" boomed Malcolm. He presented the book to the apprentice, paid, yanked open the door for his master, and followed him out to the street.

"Quick," said the wigmaker. "Fly to Madam Phipp's! Ere another suitor hands her the same book!"

Malcolm stood still. " 'Tis a worthy offering." He cast a troubled eye on the gift. "Yet I fear she may feel you've tended to her soul's nourishment but neglected her body's."

Mr. Hogwood, his own soul harassed past endurance, hurriedly searched his several pockets. "Greedy she-dragon! Add these to the tribute!" He handed his servant a half-emptied, paper-wrapped bundle of sugared almonds. "Now be off!"

Malcolm shot forward at once up the cobblestoned path worn through the snow. He turned to the right, leaving his master's sight, devoured a half dozen of the almonds, and was about to enter his favorite cookshop for a leisurely lamb chop and mug of ale when he noticed Madam Phipp's serving girl strolling a few paces ahead. Ignoring the enticing aroma of meat, he focused his mind on higher matters, adjusted his hat, smartened his coat, and discreetly advanced to her side.

"What luck! Well met! Returning to your mistress?"

The manservant's question went unanswered, as the girl, upon recognizing him, instantly doubled her speed.

"I'm bound that way myself, as it happens." He admired afresh her linen-white skin while straining to keep up with her graceful gait. "My master wishes to give a gift to Madam Phipp." He indicated the book. "I likewise have something to bestow. Upon you."

He closed up the paper bundle in his pocket, offered it, grinned, but received no response. He avoided a pair of pigs, swerved to the left to stay beside the girl, then discovered, too late, that she'd guided his feet through a mound of freshly deposited horse dung.

"Almonds!" he called out, falling behind. Frantically cleaning his boots in the snow, he returned his feet to the cobblestones, saw her turn right, and strode frenziedly after her.

"*Sugared* almonds!" the manservant panted when he'd caught up. He presented them again.

" 'Tis a crime to accept stolen goods," the girl informed him without slowing her pace.

Malcolm affected an injured look, searched his wits for an alternate explanation of how he'd come by the nuts, then suddenly saw that the girl had taken advantage of his preoccupation to lead him straight toward a hitching post. Lurching at the last moment, he tangled his legs, tripped, and went sprawling in such fashion that his right hand and the book it was holding landed in a puddle of worrisome origin located next to a butcher's cart.

Fearing to lose sight of the girl, Malcolm struggled to his feet and drained Dr. Mather's sermons while he ran. He eeled his way between passersby, dodging handcarts and wood sellers' wagons.

" 'Twas a gift from Mr. Hogwood! To mark my birthday!" He caught up with her just as she reached Madam Phipp's. And was gratified to see the girl finally stop, turn, glance demurely at her feet, then raise her smiling eyes toward his.

"Truly."

"In faith!" wheezed Malcolm, out of breath. Though the statement was false, its parts were at least true. Wasn't his birthday in the month of December, albeit two weeks in the future? Wasn't his master's name Mr. Hogwood? "My twentieth," he added proudly.

Lowering her eyes in a modest fashion that particularly attracted him, the girl edged two paces to her left, followed like a shadow by Malcolm—who suddenly felt his feet give way and plunge through a skin of thawing ice into a thigh-deep, water-filled pothole. Struck voiceless by the cold, his arms shot up, from which convenient height the serving girl plucked the book from his fingers, declined the almonds, offered her warmest congratulations on his birthday, and marched inside.

FOUR

LATER THAT AFTERNOON Boston's weathervanes sud-
enly shifted in unison, all pointing accusingly toward
he north. An icy wind swooped down on the streets.
Clouds curtained the sun. Birds sought shelter. By
nightfall the sky had begun bestowing snow upon the
own, stingily at first, then with boundless philan-
hropy. Flakes covered the cobblestones once more,
ecolonized the windowsills, and filled portly Mr. Trul-
iber's lantern beam with a legion of alarming mirages.

The night watchman ambled up Mackerel Lane. He
isliked falling snow. Crossing King Street, he found
he normally empty thoroughfare thronged with
volves and fleeing thieves. Silent, billowing beings

51

whom he felt bound by his public duty to probe with
his light lest any prove real.

Glancing down an alleyway, he trained his beam
on the shape of a serving girl sprinting with a strongbox
in her arms. He shouted out to her to halt and watched
as the flakes of which she was made obediently fell
to earth. Walking on, he certified the insubstantiality
of scores of dicers, dancers, arsonists, Indians, papists,
witches, and sundry other threats to the public peace.
Then he glimpsed the outline of a boy standing in
front of an apothecary's shop, a figure who failed to
dissolve.

"You! State your business!"

There came no reply. A gust whipped snow into
the watchman's face, blinding him for a moment.
"Stand fast!" Fearing the boy would dash away, he
lumbered toward him, squinting through the flakes,
holding his lantern out at arm's length—and discovered
that he'd been addressing a sundial.

He glared at the column upon which it was mounted,
falling snow accumulating on his hat, shoulders, and
ample stomach. He searched for any witnesses to his
folly, then aimed his light upon the dial, brushed off
the snow, and made out the words "The Hour Is At
Hand." He sneered. A poor choice of motto, he mused,
to place before a shop selling medicines. And if the
hour were indeed at hand, the sundial gave no indica-
tion. Once the sun set it could show *no* hour, slumber-
ing like the rest of the town. The sleep-scorning Mr.
Trulliber eyed the timepiece with lordly contempt.
Tapping its granite pillar with his toe, he reconfirmed

hat it was not a boy's leg, turned, marched on, and ailed to spy a boy not of stone but of flesh dart across he street just half a block to his rear.

William paused, made certain of the watchman's course, hurried on—then froze. Footsteps were coming! Panicked, he flattened himself against a recessed shop door and seconds later sensed a moving human presence inches away: Bootheels sounded, clothing rustled, the faint breeze from the walker's passage brushed against his face. He heard a man's voice, humming jauntily.

Mr. Baggot, the tithingman! William's heart boomed. Even though he'd excused the apprentice from his twice-weekly examinations, the man had been much on William's mind. Twice he'd thought he'd glimpsed him lurking outside Mr. Currie's after dark, waiting to snare him, as he'd vowed to do. "I want you to know that my eye is upon you." His words reverberated in William's mind. And yet, the voice of the man who'd just passed seemed higher than Mr. Baggot's. . . .

William waited, stepped out from the door, and saw no sign of the man. He sped on, reached Boston's North End, and blew upon his fingers. Putting his heron-bone flute to his lips, he began to play, shaping his breath into tunes that led his mind to wander back to winters long past. Through the veil of falling snow he could almost believe that the water on his right was not Boston Harbor but Narragansett Bay, that the buildings about him were his tribe's winter houses, that the long-handled pump ahead was in fact his father crouching, stringing a bow. If he found a road leading back to his former life, would he take it? He pondered the question. The English were greedy, ruthless, self-righteous, fearfully serving a god who was as cruel a master as the worst who walked Boston. Yet he now spoke, wrote, thought, and dreamed in their language as naturally as swallows swooped through the air. He was held up as a shining example of hard work and quick wits—a model for the very people who'd murdered his family.

He turned from the harbor and strolled up an alley. It wasn't often that he wandered the town twice within a fortnight. But the note that morning, and the news that another Narraganset servant had come to the North End, had drawn him back out into the streets. His music quivered with readiness. He felt that a meeting lay before him.

He angled down North Street, his eyes flitting from window to window, then scouting for watchmen. The snow was falling more thickly now, seeming to occupy all the air, a silent torrent that hid William from sight but left his music free to tap gently at windows and to curl underneath doors. He reached the wharves again and turned north. Twice he made out Cancasset's face behind a window, only to find that the falling snow had deceived him. His path meandering, he strolled up one street and doubled back down another. He passed Hudson's Point and the burying place. He wound alongside the Charles River. He trudged past churches, shipyards, the Battery. Finally, he leaned up against a cooper's door to rest.

He'd been awake since cockcrow, as usual, and had

a full day in the printing room ahead. And all of a sudden he felt footsore, weary as a mill horse, ravenous for sleep. He'd been mad to think he would find Cancasset. Frequently his flute had lured to a window or door a Narraganset servant who was unknown to him, but not even that had happened this night.

Reluctantly straightening up, he staggered homeward like a sleepwalker. His cloak was as white as the coat of a hare. Turning to his left down Middle Street, he warmed his frigid fingers and piped himself toward bed with a lullaby he remembered hearing his father play, then slowed his feet. Then stopped entirely.

A window to his right had suddenly brightened. William played on a few moments, then softened his flute, then silenced it altogether. The light came from a dilapidated shed. Its single window was missing most of its panes of glass, through which opening he clearly made out the outline of a face.

He approached, braced to flee should he need to. The flickering within revealed to him that the figure's forehead was high. Then that the ears and chin were long. Then that the face belonged to a male, who commenced to hum the rest of the tune that William had broken off. In astonishment, the apprentice listened. He came closer. And found himself staring, amazed, at his own father's uncle.

He felt unsteady, like the light within. "Michamauk," he called out, too loudly he realized.

The man's eyes grew huge, glowing like a cat's. "Who are you?" he asked in Narraganset.

The words were both foreign and familiar to William.

For an instant, his spinning brain was unable to remember his former name.

"Weetasket!" he burst out at last.

His great-uncle's eyes narrowed, as if in disbelief, then expanded again. Then he turned and drew away from the window. William made out a sound nearby. Circling the building, he caught sight of a hand reaching out through a gap between boards and inserting a key into the heavy padlock that secured the shed's door. The lock sprang open and was lifted from the latch by the disembodied hand. Stepping forward, the apprentice slowly opened the squealing door—and gawked. The hand wasn't Michamauk's but a girl's.

"Who is this?" he asked in English, then put the words into Narraganset, surprised that his memory supplied them so quickly.

"Ninnomi," his great-uncle replied. He adjusted the guttering wick in his lamp and held it beside her. "Your cousin."

In the suddenly stronger light, William studied the old man, tall but unstooped, white-haired, wrinkled, missing several more teeth than he remembered. Then he turned to the young girl beside him and picked her up in his arms. She'd been a wailing infant the last time he'd seen her. Grasping for words, he told her who he was. Then he broke off suddenly and faced his great-uncle.

"Where is Cancasset?"

The man's long, lined face stiffened. "That is not a name to be spoken, Weetasket."

William lowered Ninnomi to the floor, puzzling over the reply. He comprehended the words but not their meaning. Then he understood. It was forbidden to utter the names of the dead.

"Your brother was sent to Barbados, as a slave." Michamauk hung the lamp near the window. "For stealing an Englishman's gun."

William stood stiffly, as if he were one of the company of the dead himself. Dazed, he thought back to the days when he and Cancasset had hidden from the English in the woods, and recalled his brother's pride at snatching the musket from a sleeping soldier.

"Soon after he landed he tried to escape from the sugar fields, from the men with the whips. He was caught, and shot dead. I learned of this during the past year's fruit moon."

William stood, unspeaking, while the impossible fact unfolded in his mind. Each time he'd gazed into a looking glass and believed he was viewing Cancasset, he'd been wrong. He'd deluded himself, willingly, for six years. When the thought had sprung up that Cancasset might be dead, he'd dismissed it, picturing him in Plymouth, or Canada, or somewhere in the lands west of the English. Each time he'd wondered about Cancasset, he'd imagined Cancasset wondering about him. And each time he'd been wrong. The looking glass had held no one but himself.

"He lives with our forefathers," said Michamauk. Slowly, he bent his long legs and sat down on some straw, Ninnomi beside him. "In the house of Cautantowwit, the creator. To the southwest, where the air is always mild."

William sat upon the dirt floor, only half listening to the old man's account of his snatching up tiny Ninnomi and escaping the village, set afire by the English, of their six years serving a brutish Plymouth gunsmith, his sudden death, and their purchase by Mr. Rudd.

The apprentice emerged from his trance with a start. "*Mr. Rudd*? The maker of eyeglasses?" He thought of their meeting that morning and prayed that the town held another man by that name.

His great-uncle nodded and William jumped up. Glancing outside, it dawned on him that he had indeed been walking down Middle Street and that Mr. Rudd's shop must be next door. He surveyed the room, bare except for two scatterings of straw to sleep upon, the room that so many apprentices had fled. "The man is a tyrant." He'd had to search for the word, knew he was making mistakes in his former language, but plunged ahead. "Has he beaten you?"

"He has a whip," said Michamauk. "With three cords. We have both felt it once."

"And the awl," spoke Ninnomi.

"The awl?" The apprentice cocked his head, then recalled that Mr. Rudd had brandished one in the shop that morning.

"It hangs by a cord from his neck," said Michamauk. "He uses it to scratch the proper age of wearer into the glass of each pair of spectacles."

58

"And to jab us when he believes we're idle." The girl displayed two wounds on her arm.

William seethed. "What work has he given you?"

"Ninnomi keeps his house. I stand and grind glass."

"Does he feed you?"

"One hard roll at noontime." Michamauk grunted. "A wormy apple perhaps. The dogs in the street find more to eat."

William searched his pockets and offered a potato skin and two scraps of cheese rind, intended for those same street dogs.

"I can bring you more," he said. "Much more." He saw how quickly they snapped up the food, how thoroughly they licked their fingers, and he cursed the eyeglass maker.

"How did you get the rogue's key?" he asked.

"Ninnomi found it under the straw. Carved from wood and left for us. Perhaps by the man's last apprentice."

"And why don't you leave in the night?" asked William.

Michamauk filled a stone pipe with tobacco. "How I would like to do just that. To find myself back among the budding trees during this year's green moon." He lit his pipe from the lamp and inhaled deeply, the scent of tobacco mixing with lamp's odor of burning deer fat. "But Mr. Rudd says that we'll never escape him. That he has eyeglasses that allow a man to see for fifty miles."

William had heard of Tut's telescope. "The man lies," he stated nevertheless. "He wishes to hold you with fear." Then he noticed that the lamp was hanging near the window. "Will he not see us?" He looked fearful himself.

Michamauk shook his head. "He sleeps above the shop, in the rear. And it's he himself who gave us the lamp, to study the Bible by. We've put it to use the past two nights, not for reading, but so that I could begin to teach Ninnomi to weave. As best as I'm able to teach such things."

William spied a small pile of weed stems on the ground and an unfinished basket beside them, then looked up at his great-uncle. Though dressed in the Englishmen's breeches and shirt and shoes, the man within seemed unchanged. He still spoke Narraganset, still reckoned time by the Narraganset moons, still sucked on a stone pipe in the evening. With no mother to instruct Ninnomi, he was teaching her basket-weaving—women's work—so that she should make a good Narraganset wife. The girl got up to watch the snow through the window, and suddenly the apprentice realized that Michamauk had been studying him as well.

"I see, Weetasket, that you wear false hair on your head," he said. "Like the other coatmen."

It had been many years since he'd heard the Narragansets' word for the English settlers. William's eyes fell. "Yes, Great-uncle."

"And that your tongue stumbles in speaking your own language."

William felt shamed. "Yes, great-uncle. Six years now I've lived among the English."

"As has Ninnomi," Michamauk added curtly. "She has learned the language of the coatmen without forgetting a word of her own."

William paused to show respect. "She's been fortunate to have you to speak with."

Michamauk sucked on his pipe, ruminating. "I see too that your clothes are very fine. Your master must be a man of importance."

"Yes!" spoke up William. "Mr. Currie, the printer." Grateful for a chance to defend himself, he launched into a description of the Currie family, the life of the printer's shop, the praise he'd received for his typesetting and his studies. Lest Michamauk think he'd abandoned his own kind, he produced the flute whose music they'd heard, played his three tunes, and recounted his countless night wanderings in search of Cancasset.

His great-uncle puffed on his pipe while he spoke. Ninnomi, stationed in front of the window, turned her head from the falling snow to listen to her cousin's account. While, outside in the street, a passerby halted abruptly and stood transfixed, staring at the window as if he too were enthralled by William's tale.

Spellbound, Mr. Speke peered before him. He couldn't make out the apprentice's words, nor could he glimpse him within. What he saw was an illuminated window, a tiny land of light, the sole sign of life, it seemed, in all of Boston. And within that window he saw a head turned in profile, the head of a girl, clearly visible through the missing panes. A girl whose

61

features struck him at once as Indian, perhaps Narra-ganset.

The wood-carver quietly moved two paces closer through the snow. Utterly rapt, he studied her face. Her forehead was high, and most handsome, he thought. Her chin was short. Her hair was braided. She looked seven or eight years old, about the same age as the girl whose shriek haunted him. And though he stood as stiffly as if turned to granite, he felt, to the contrary, brought to life, felt raised from the grave that had been his spirit's home for the past several months. In the midst of winter, his own and the world's, he thought that he scented spring.

Absolutely still, oblivious of the snow, he gazed upon her face for a quarter hour. Then she moved out of view. The carver kept his place. He didn't wish to walk directly up to the window and possibly frighten her. And he'd seen all that he needed to see. She was a providence, sent to fill his need. Trembling, though not with the cold, he backed away from the shed.

He'd return, he vowed. The first thing in the morning! He would place his proposition to her master!

Glowing inside, as if the girl had kindled a fire within him, Mr. Speke struck out down Middle Street, light-footed, light-headed, his mind racing. And thus un-likely to have noticed, across the street and tucked into an alleyway, the all-but-invisible outline of a man. A young man watching Mr. Rudd's shop and shed, his mind likewise busy, and his mouth as well, occu-pied with humming a lively tune.

62

FIVE

SOMETIME IN THE NIGHT the snow stopped falling, at an hour known only to the watchmen. At nine the next morning a coach-and-four snorted and jangled through the whitened town, scattering pigs and persons alike, and halted abruptly before Mr. Currie's, an event by contrast, known to nearly all of upper King Street.

Giles, Madam Phipp's footman, hopped from the back of the coach and opened her door. A towering woman, dressed in mourning black from hood to shawl to shoes, she missed the coach's bottom step, plunged her left foot into the snow, and proceeded to curse her footman, then the coach's maker, then Mr. Rudd, who'd sold her on the previous day the brass-rimmed glasses affixed to her face, aids to sight that rendered the world a good deal blurrier than she recalled it.

"This way, Madam." Giles guided her. Short, portly, ablaze in red livery, the footman opened the printer's door for her. Though she preferred to make her own purchases, he decided to follow his mistress inside, thinking that she might need his assistance, and was informed to the contrary by means of a sharp crack on his knuckles from her brass-ribbed fan, an article she carried in all seasons for that purpose.

Upon hearing the shop's bell, William entered and found the woman squinting about at the walls as if she weren't sure where she was.

"I shall be giving a dinner a few days hence," Madam Phipp mumbled hazily. She turned toward the boy, then wondered whether she wasn't facing a stepladder instead. "To mark the end of my mourning time."

"I see," the apprentice replied.

Wishing she could make the same claim, the woman turned to her right toward his voice. "On the twenty-second, to be exact."

"Yes, Madam." William noted that the Curries' Saturnalia would take place that same day.

Straining to determine precisely where he was, Madam Phipp suddenly suspected that the apprentice was staring at her, then was struck by the sight of a hen on a shelf. Emptied of patience with her spectacles, she angrily ridded her eyes of them, found she'd been viewing a mug filled with quills, and vowed to wear the lying, vile lenses no more than an hour a day—some other hour than this one.

"I'll need ink for invitations!" she declared. "I'll require paper! And more sealing wax!" As if the fog had suddenly lifted from her mind as well as her eyes, she directed a volley of orders toward William, paid for her purchases, strode out the door, and struck Giles smartly on the ear for not listening for her steps and opening it for her.

William watched her coach depart, then sold one copy of an apprenticeship contract to a humming young man whose low-brimmed black hat nearly obscured his eyes, sea-green eyes that lit in sudden surprise at the sight of William.

Returning to the printing room, the apprentice resumed receiving instruction from Mr. Currie on the craft of binding books. Mrs. Currie, behind them, was busy at setting type, Gwenne at trimming lamp wicks, and Amos at singing and inking the press. Having finished his quizzing of the Currie children, Mr. Baggot joined the company.

He cleared his throat. "Young Timothy, sir, is neglecting his Bible," he addressed the printer. "The rod of correction is sorely needed."

Mr. Currie glanced up, then returned to drawing his needle and thread through the pages he was stitching.

"While Sarah's bearing has grown most saucy. I fear she has put on Satan's jeweled crown."

The room's other occupants continued at their tasks, Amos refusing to give up his song. The tithingman tightened his grip on his staff.

"Further, my ears receive grave reports. Tales of a pagan celebration in which master and servant exchange their stations and all authority is mocked. A heathenish outrage, depraved and unchristian."

"Most Christian, in fact," answered Mr. Currie. "A brief bringing to earth of the kingdom of Heaven. Where, as you know, the last shall be first."

Stung speechless, the tithingman hunted a reply. Then he cast his eyes upon William.

"I've a word to speak on your apprentice as well." He crossed the room and stood staring at William. "A dutiful scholar. Ever prepared. Possessed of a powerful memory for Scripture." He paused until all heads had lifted in curiosity at these compliments. "But don't think that his memory doesn't hold more. Such as the art of hacking Christians to death while they sleep—as my grandsons were slain!"

Before William's defenders could speak, Mr. Baggot strode briskly out of the room. He slammed the front door and turned up King Street, bringing his bootheels down on the snow as if on the throat of an enemy. He would snare the boy, just as he'd vowed. Tomorrow he'd pay an Indian wench to approach the apprentice and beg him to slip her one of the printer's silver tankards, that she might buy food for her sore-stomached young. He smiled at his own cleverness. Fervently, he prayed to God to deliver the tawny into his hand, and promised in return that the knave would be chastised in this world as well as the next. Picturing with pleasure the overeducated Indian being flogged, then pelted in the stocks, then hanged, the tithingman neared Mr. Hogwood's shop, glared at the ungodly wigs in the window, and appended his prayer with the wish that the wigmaker, and all his ilk, might be destroyed as well.

This request was countered by Mr. Hogwood's own, that the Lord might empty the vials of his wrath on the wig-hating tithingman passing his window. Confident that the Almighty stood with him on the wig-wearing controversy, and most likely sported one Himself, Mr. Hogwood peered hopefully through the glass, waiting for his petition to be answered.

"Uncle! The cat's left another mouse head!"

Mr. Hogwood whirled toward his nephew, Dan, proudly displaying the trophy in his hand. "And don't you possess a head of your own? Away with it! Now! Ere a customer comes!"

The wigmaker turned back to the window and found he could no longer see Mr. Baggot. Had he walked out of view or been felled by the Lord? Cursing Dan, he stepped over to the hearth and stared at the flames, pondering his troubles. His exasperating nephew had no more sense than a head of cabbage. Mr. Weems, the judge, his most prominent patron, had yesterday morning found fault with his wigs and informed Mr. Hogwood that he would have them dressed elsewhere. That afternoon he'd set eyes on a pamphlet claiming the Indian attacks six years back were God's punishment for putting on wigs. And then there was Malcolm, his manservant. One of the kegs of beer he was brewing had burst in the cellar that morning, making a mess he'd refused to clean up, insisting that the task was beneath him. Next, he'd declined to clear the snow from before the shop, declaring that his domain did not reach beyond the front door. Finally, and most worrisome, the scamp had chanced to mention that Madam Phipp was soon to come out of mourning—and that the suitors would then be thick as flies.

How did his manservant come by this news? God alone knew all, yet Malcolm seemed to be apprised of scarcely less. The wigmaker turned and surveyed his shop. Apprentices and journeymen were busy snipping, combing, curling. Mr. Hogwood's vexed mind, however, was fixed not upon hair, but the heart.

"Malcolm!" he shouted with sudden resolution. Knowing that his servant never appeared until summoned no less than four times, he put the interval to use by taking out quill, ink, and paper, called him several more times while writing, fetched a tiny ivory box, beckoned him again, at greater volume, took up one of Madam Phipp's servant's wigs, and finally shrieked his name one more time, unaware that Malcolm was now at his side.

"Did you ask for me, sir?" the manservant inquired.

Not deigning to reply, Mr. Hogwood thrust a wig box into his arms. He placed the wig inside, then added the card upon which he'd written "With the Special Compliments of Samuel Hogwood, Wigmaker, King Street, Boston."

"Carry it to Madam Phipp." He then plucked the ivory box from his pocket, took out the gold-edged locket inside, opened it, frowned at the portrait of Cupid, then placed it back in its box. His father had presented the locket to his mother. Based on that record of success, and his servant's advice to appeal to the widow's feminine nature, he handed it to Malcolm. "Give her this also. And be quick about it!"

Exiting through the rear of the shop, Malcolm took the liberty of exchanging his battered woolen hat for one of Mr. Hogwood's sleek beavers. As instructed, he made his way through the streets as speedily as he could, though not in the direction of Madam Phipp's. Entering a small shop near Say's wharf, he traded the wigmaker's gold-chained locket for two others of lesser value, hurried on to the widow's house, and was disappointed when the door was opened not by her thin serving girl but rather by her thick footman, Giles.

The man eyed Malcolm. "What's your business?" he croaked.

Looking over his head, Malcolm scanned the house, searching for the girl. "I've a wig to deliver," he answered the footman absently. "From Mr. Hogwood." He gave the wig box to the man, who proceeded to shut the door.

"Hold! There's more!" Malcolm fished through his pockets and extracted a slightly dented locket, missing its chain and bearing the mysterious initials "W. Y." within. "A gift for Madam Phipp. From my master." He handed the trinket to the footman and quickly placed the other locket in the wigmaker's ivory box. "Mr. Hogwood wished me also to convey a message to the serving girl here. She with brown hair and blue eyes."

The man appeared doubtful. "In faith, did he now?"

He smiled sourly at Malcolm. "You may tell *Mr. Hogwood* that the girl is busy upstairs at her work. As you ought to be also!"

He slammed the door.

Malcolm stepped back. Looking up at the second-floor windows, he worked his way along the front of the house, crippling several seedling trees. He rounded a corner, craning his neck, and passed around a chimney. Then he glimpsed her.

He tossed a pebble at the window and waved. He straightened Mr. Hogwood's hat, composed his thoughts, and readied himself. First, he would discover where she was from, then reveal that he'd been born there as well. This striking connection between them established, he'd next present the locket, briefly recounting its long history in his family. Following this, he would set forth his ambitions once his service had ended, impressing upon her the earnestness of his—

The window opened.

"Good day!" he called up. He smiled, then cleared his throat. "With all submission, is it true, as I've heard, that you come from the county of Hampshire, the most beautiful in—"

At that moment, a waterfall of filth from a chamber pot, quite large and quite full, descended upon the manservant, drenching his face and Mr. Hogwood's hat, fouling his waistcoat, running down his back, and conveying, he believed, the message that the girl was not from Hampshire, that she was occupied with her chores, and that she'd prefer to take up the subject another time.

Favoring a recess himself, Malcolm departed in search of a pump.

"Penny a peep!" shouted out Tut. The sky that evening had been swept clean of clouds. A vast chandelier of stars sparkled overhead, while up from the waters the moon was emerging. "Gaze on the wonders of God's firmament!"

He patted his dog, who was lying on the snow, wound up tightly against the cold. He looked down Deer Lane, then up Middle Street, at the intersection of which thoroughfares he'd set up his telescope with high hopes. Expectantly, he scanned the lit windows of the several taverns and cookshops nearby, then trained his instrument on the moon, rising over the horizon like the huge eye of a cyclops, wide with curiosity.

"Behold the moon's every hill and hare!" he bellowed. "Penny a peep!"

Five men exited from a tavern. The tallest of them veered toward Tut, gave him a coin, and put his eye to the telescope.

"Do you make out the man?" Tut asked him.

"The man?"

"In the moon. There in the center of the glass." His patron's companions clustered about.

"Truly," the man mumbled. He switched eyes and squinted.

"Banished above for gathering wood on the Sabbath," added Tut. "So 'tis said."

"Faith, yes," his customer declared. "I warrant I spy him out pretty clear."

One of the other men paid his fare. Not wishing to be thought a fool, he agreed that the moon did indeed hold a man, relating to the rest some details of his dress, an account confirmed and added to by each of the remaining three men.

The five ambled off, Tut fingering their coins. It was early still, yet he'd already brought in nearly half a shilling. He surveyed his new location with approval. An excellent choice, he complimented himself, then made out the sound of feet.

"Behold the man in the moon!" he called out. "Plain as a plow horse! Penny a peep!"

The couple approaching ignored this enticement. One tall and broad-shouldered, the other quite small, they passed him, turned down Bartholomew Street, and stamped the snow from their shoes before the door of a narrow shop.

"My wife has prepared you some food," said Mr. Speke. The carver led Ninnomi inside, the air suddenly smelling of pine, as if the door opened onto a forest. They filed through a low room crowded with wood in every form, from post to peg, the floor wearing a winter coat of wood shavings. Beyond lay the living quarters, where Mr. Speke seated the girl at a table holding turnips, hashed mutton, brown bread, and cider. The wood-carver left to fetch another lamp and returned to find her devouring the meal. Scant wonder, he mused, that Mr. Rudd had so quickly agreed to give up the girl for the evening in exchange for Mr. Speke's feeding her supper. He'd likely not cast her a crumb all day.

The carver threw more wood on the fire, positioned the lamps on either side of Ninnomi, then brought to the table pen, ink, and paper.

"Pay me no thought," he almost whispered. He dipped his pen into the inkhorn and began to sketch her left profile, struggling to keep his hand from trembling. His quill scratched roughly on the paper, leaving behind the line of her brow, then her nose and lips, then her delicate chin. He noticed that his heart was pounding. Though he'd carved figureheads before, they'd always been posed for by ship owners' wives or daughters, models who'd meant nothing to him. Mr. Epp, anxious to launch his new brig and having no female relations on hand, had left the choice of subject to Mr. Speke. After weeks of being pestered by the man, the carver had finally found one, an Indian girl of the same tribe and age as the one whose face he hadn't glimpsed but whose scream still sounded in his memory. At last he would exorcise his tormentor! A task impossible without Ninnomi's features to complete the figure.

Mr. Speke moved to her other side. "How old would you be?"

She swallowed a mouthful. "Eight years, sir. Less one month."

He began to draw her right profile, his mind suddenly fixed on his daughter. Dora had been only three when she'd died, had never grown tall like this girl at his table. He asked himself once again why the Lord had chosen to snip short her life. He was unable to keep from calculating that she would have turned four in exactly a fortnight. Or to drive from his thoughts another anniversary: six years before, to the very day, he'd been marching through the snows of Rhode Island with the rest of General Winslow's men, nearing the Narragansets' stronghold, nearing the very girl before him. . . .

Marching through the Boston snow, passing by Mr. Speke's front door, William clutched his cloak about him, then crossed the lane to avoid a passerby. It was early still and the streets weren't yet empty. Not wishing to keep his hungry great-uncle and cousin waiting until late, he'd told Mr. Currie that he'd a book to return to Mr. Leghorn, his tutor in Latin, had filled his pockets with food, and set off.

He turned onto Middle Street, passed Tut by, looked up at the moon but made out no sign of anyone looking back. A minute later he reached Mr. Rudd's. He scanned the man's windows and found them dark. Quietly, he crept around to the rear of the shed. He tapped at the door. Michamauk let him in.

"I've brought food," William said in Narraganset. He produced from his pockets two turnips, an apple, a heel of bread, and half a cake of maple sugar. "I'll try to bring more tomorrow night."

Michamauk's eyes and nostrils opened wide. He viewed the food by the light of the lamp, explained that Ninnomi was feasting as well, carried the bounty to his bed of straw, sat down, and began with the bread.

"I would have brought more," William spoke up. "But I mustn't make my mistress suspicious." Sud-

74

denly he was swept by a wave of guilt for stealing from her kitchen and brazenly lying to Mr. Currie. They'd have loaded his arms with food if he'd asked. But he hadn't wished to reveal his night searches, or give any hint that a part of him remained loyal to his past and would never step into the cheerful confines of the Currie household.

"Sit down and speak to me, Weetasket."

William impatiently shuffled his feet. "I would like to, Great-uncle. But I told my master I'd be away from the house but a short time."

Michamauk picked up one of the turnips. "Perhaps then I will speak to you." He stood up slowly and gazed out the window. "Can you name that constellation?"

William approached and followed the line of his finger. "Orion," he proudly replied. "The mightiest hunter of all the Greeks. Who was felled in turn by a goddess's arrow."

Michamauk appeared unimpressed. "So it is that the coatmen believe," he said. "Give me its name in our own language."

Desperately, William searched his mind, knowing that the name wasn't there. "I've forgotten, Great-uncle."

"I'll tell it to you," Michamauk replied. Meaningfully, he stared at William. "That and much else you ought to know. Stay awhile."

William stayed.

At nine o'clock the curfew bell rang. Those who

75

were out hastened toward home. Those who were home covered the coals in their hearths with ashes for the night. One by one, windows fell dark. Middle Street, its snow glowing in the moonlight, soon grew empty, a fact sadly noted by Tut. He counted his coins by his main attraction's light, proudly reported the night's profit to his dog, and had begun to unfasten the telescope from its wooden stand when he heard feet behind him.

"Penny a peep!" he called out, reattaching the instrument. "View the man in the moon!"

Mr. Baggot halted. " 'Tis past curfew," he barked.

Tut paled. Would he again be summoned before a judge? "So it is, in faith! And I'm off like a bird!" He returned to hurriedly loosening the nut that bound the telescope to its stand.

"Hold, sir." The tithingman, heading home after an evening of inspecting taverns, found his eye snagged by the sole lit window ahead of him on Middle Street. "A penny you say?"

"Yes, sir! But a penny!" At once, Tut's fingers changed direction again, tightening the telescope down. "And the moon man's up above, mark my word. Hauling his bundle of wood on his back." Tut cleaned the eyepiece with his handkerchief. "As befits the sinner!" he added, hoping to show himself an upholder of the law. "Would that the lot of Sabbath-breakers were transported—"

Mr. Baggot grabbed the telescope, and to its owner's amazement aimed it not up at the moon but down

76

the street. It was his sworn duty, the tithingman reminded himself, to watch over his town, to search out evil, that it might be plucked out. He caught sight of the eyeglass maker's shop and was startled by its nearness in the glass. Then he fixed his gaze on the lamp-lit window, and beheld two heads, one old, one young.

"God's wounds!" he muttered.

Tut eyed his patron, then squinted at the window, to no avail. "Saturn is out as well," he piped up, feeling left out. "Bright as a pin."

Mr. Baggot made no reply to this, or to subsequent advertisements for the splendors of Mars, the Pole Star, and Sirius. Without warning, he drew his head back from the glass, paid his penny, and scurried down the street.

Halting before he reached Mr. Rudd's, he pressed himself back into the shadows. He saw a girl enter the shed. He waited. Long after Tut had passed him, he heard the door open, made out footsteps, then saw William emerge into the street.

It was him! Without doubt! The tithingman blinked, hardly believing the sight was real. He'd snared him, in the midst of some evildoing! What need was there to set traps for the knave? "For he is cast into a net by his own feet," he recited to himself from the Bible.

Unbreathing, he watched the boy pass by. Wondering where he was headed next, he waiting until he'd turned a corner. Then he dashed through the snow, unaware that he too was being watched by a resident of the shadows, a restless man, constantly humming, his vision roofed by his hat's low brim, a man whose thoughts kept him from sleep. Thoughts focused upon none of the figures mysteriously coming and going that night, but upon a man he'd sworn he would revisit one day—the sleeping Mr. Rudd.

SIX

FOUR MORNINGS LATER Mr. Currie and his wife were awakened by the beating of a drum outside their chamber.

"Rise up!" demanded a voice. "Up sharp!"

The sky was just beginning to brighten. It was December twenty-second, the winter solstice—and the day of the Saturnalia.

"Out of bed, do you hear! Sleep-guzzling sluggards!" A hand, then several, pounded on the door. One of them flung it open and the room rattled with the beating of the drum, the clanging of pot lids, and the shrilling of whistles as William, the serving girl Gwenne, and five of the Curries' children paraded inside, waking the sixth, the infant Rose, who slept in a cradle beside her parents and whose crying joined the cacophony.

" 'Tis nigh upon noon!" shouted out Sarah. She motioned to the others to cease their noisemaking.

"The morning star's already set!" declared William.

"Hours ago!" lisped Timothy.

"There's a world of chores waiting!" cried Gwenne. "And behold the lag-lasts! Lolling in bed!"

At this, the entire company rushed upon the printer and his wife, threw off their blankets and cattail-fluff quilt, and drove them from the fort of their four-poster.

"There's water needs fetching!"

"And the fires to kindle!"

"And breakfast to get for your hungry masters!"

The two masters-turned-servants, feigning worry for their lives, hurriedly jumped into their clothes and were hounded downstairs by the clamoring throng. Mrs. Currie lugged water from the pump in leather buckets. Her husband hauled wood inside from the shed, raked the ashes off the night's embers, and blew on the cluster of surviving coals to start the new day's fires. The journeyman Amos, who lodged nearby, arrived and added his orders to the others'. Presently, Mr. Currie served breakfast, and was made to beg his betters' pardon for its lateness, meagerness, and poor quality. After they'd eaten he disappeared, returning, as he did each year, bearing a custard pie, baked the night before and containing somewhere inside it a pea-sized wooden crown. He cut it into equal-sized pieces.

"Rachel's is wider, 'tis plain!"

"So is Ruth's!"

"I've never once reigned! Mine ought to be larger!"

The printer placed slices before everyone but himself nd his wife and watched the group eat. For the first ime that day they were silent, preoccupied with carefully chewing each bite.

" 'Tis in mine!" shrieked a voice.

All heads turned toward Gwenne, who extracted rom her mouth the miniature crown and held it up or all to see.

"Queen Gwenne!" proclaimed Mr. Currie. He kneeled before her. "Monarch of mischief!"

"Queen Gwenne!" the others repeated in unison.

Beaming, the serving girl decreed that her subjects had leave to finish their pie. When they had, a fine ribbon of royal purple was passed through the center of the crown, and the emblem of her rule, much indented with the toothmarks of previous sovereigns, was solemnly lowered over her head.

"May Saturn's reign return this day," Mr. Currie earnestly intoned. "A golden age, without war, without vant. A time with neither masters nor slaves, when ll sowed and reaped side by side. A time of pleasure nd plenty!"

"Plenty of rum!" burst out Amos, and the celebration vas launched. Those passersby who found that the hop was closed, presumably in mourning, were surprised by the quantity, and character, of the noise coming from within. Following the ancient Romans, Mr. Currie set out a supply of liquors: rum, beer, cherry brandy, syllabub, and Canary wine. Amos tuned his fiddle and played. Forbidden games of cards and dice indulged in only on this day, produced a year's store of whoops and groans. Gifts were exchanged. Songs were sung. Pranks planned months before were sprung. Presiding over all, and making the most of her reign, which would expire at midnight, Gwenne set her subjects hopping to commands that mocked all exercise of power.

"William! Imitate the walking of a goose!"

"Ruth! Sing 'Heart's Ease' while balanced on your head!"

"Sarah! Stand on a chair and dispraise yourself for all to hear!"

Mr. Currie was bid to scrub the dirtied dishes with snow instead of sand. His wife was ordered to pluck a live chicken. Both were endlessly scolded with false ferocity from every quarter.

"Dough head! Are you blind? Do you find this mug clean?"

"Leap to it!"

"And no napping while you're about it!"

"Cheeky, straw-brained, slothful servants!"

At half past twelve, dinner was served. Always the day's most substantial meal, on this one day a year it became a true feast, prepared and humbly placed before the household's new masters by Mr. Currie, faithful to Roman tradition. Barbs ceased to stream from the youngsters' mouths as they watched the flotilla of well-laden plates and tureens sail in from the kitchen. There

82

was turkey and mutton and roast venison. There was salmon and cod, oysters and eels, olives and raisins and pumpkin bread. Followed by marzipan, mince pie, rumcake, and hot spiced wine for all. It was a meal the memory of which would help to carry them through the winter, through the salted, pickled, cellared fare they would stare at until fresh greens came in spring. It was therefore not devoured dog-style, but sniffed and savored, treasured on the tongue, a meal that was still being consumed when the church bell struck the hour of two.

Mr. Speke dined not at all that noon, and had taken only bread and milk that morning. For several days he'd scarcely eaten, his body as well as his soul engrossed in fashioning the figurehead.

He stood before it now, eyeing his rendering of Ninnomi's features. The past four evenings she'd come to his house. Although he'd no longer needed her presence once he'd sketched her face, he'd felt driven to feed her, all she could hold, to bandage the new wound from Mr. Rudd's awl, to send her back more warmly dressed against the winter cold than she'd come. During that time he'd progressed from sketches to a model to the full-sized figurehead, six feet high, a single piece of white pine that stood in the center of his shop. Wood chips had collected at its base as he'd shaped a high-cheeked head, then braided hair, then the slender body of a girl. He'd worked furiously, filled with energy never elicited by requests for signboards or chests or chairs. His widest chisels had given way to those narrower, then to those smaller still. The evening before, he'd filed the wood, then sanded, then begun to paint it. Returning to the task this morning, he'd now finished everything but the face.

He touched his brush to the black on his palette and outlined one of the girl's eyebrows. Much taller than most, he found it strange to stare into eyes that were level with his own. He recharged his brush. The carving's skin had already been given Ninnomi's bronze hue. He finished the eyebrow, painted its mate, stepped back, and felt his heart gaining speed. The face was emerging from the world of wood. He added black lashes, whitened the eyes' whites, and gave the pupils Ninnomi's deep brown. He scouted her braid of black hair for flaws. Taking up another brush, he reddened her lips, dabbed at her brow, and subtly colored her cheeks and chin.

He stood back and stared, his heart galloping now. The figure's eyes glistened. The face seemed of flesh. He half believed it was indeed the screaming girl's, and suddenly he felt unsteady on his feet, felt that she was present before him, and found himself cast back to the past: to the winter march on the Narragansets, the loathing he'd shared with the other men for the brutish, barbarous enemy, the sighting of their village hidden on an island in the marshland known as the Great Swamp. So well hidden it would never have been found but for the help of a traitor to the tribe. An utterly invulnerable refuge, but for the past week's

Hell-chilling cold—so fierce that the swamp had frozen solid. The tawnies' cooking fires scented the air. They were tending to their suppers, not their muskets. The carver crossed the ice with the others, burst into the village, shot one brave, then was driven out with the other soldiers. Fighting his way back in among the wigwams, he was ordered to set them afire. He hesitated, protesting that they could offer the troops shelter from the cold. The officer, enraged, repeated the order. He obeyed, and in minutes the village of branches and bark had become an inferno. The air filled with smoke and screams. Women and children and men too old to fight had been hiding by the hundreds in their houses, surprised by the English, too terrified to flee. Reloading his flintlock amid the panic, he noticed a girl with a wooden ladle, clutched as a weapon or to beat back the flames, watched her dash wildly away, her clothes and hair blazing, her face unseen but her shriek pulsing in his ears. . . .

Mr. Speke tried to shake himself free of the memory. Struggling to return to the present, he reapproached the carving of the girl and searched for any further need of paint. He studied her moccasins and dress, painted light brown like the deerskin she'd worn. He viewed the belt and shell bracelet he'd recalled, inspected the arms crossed over her chest, then the hands, one of which held a ladle. He'd shrugged off the girl and her cry at the time, had forgotten about her within a few months. He'd married. Dora, his daughter, had been born. Then, this past fall, she'd been seized by smallpox. He'd nursed her through her burning fevers, had pleaded, sworn, shouted to the Lord on her last night to take him in her place. His prayer went unanswered. The child was buried. And without warning the screaming girl was back, remembered in excruciating detail, howling all night long in his head. Then it had struck him that the foes he'd cursed as animals had died with no less suffering than his Dora. That their survivors must have begged them to live, wept, wished to die too, as he had. That the screaming girl's father, if he'd lived, must have felt the same grief that gripped his own soul. Had his Dora been taken by God, he now wondered, with his own enlightenment in mind? He thought with revulsion of the glee with which the Great Swamp fight was still recounted, the joy that was taken in the tale of how in a single day New England's mightiest tribe was shattered, toppled from its throne, its people transformed from lords into servants. Some held that God had ordained that the heathen, Devil-worshipping Narragansets should be burned along with their dinners. Others spoke of the tribe's haughty independence and well-favored lands. Still others moaned of the shortage of servants, a need that Indian captives helped fill. When he heard that single scream in his ears, Mr. Speke knew none of those reasons was sufficient.

He set down his palette. He cleaned his brushes. No penance would cancel the suffering he'd caused, but he would do what he could within his compass, as he had with the figurehead before him. He'd carved a memorial for the glimpsed girl, albeit with a borrowed face—a girl who'd received neither grave nor headstone. Mr. Epp, the bow of whose brig she'd adorn, would flinch at the sight of her. But he was anxious to sail and would know full well that no crew, superstitious to a man, would cast off without a figurehead.

He turned from the carving, opened his door, and stepped out into the winter afternoon. The sky was clear, the air frigid, as it had been for several days. He viewed the sun, low, weak, and robbed of all leverage, then recalled it was the solstice. A day of change, when the celestial balance shifted toward the strengthening sun and its return to mastery of the heavens. Gazing at the pale blue sky, the carver felt that he too was moving in a new direction, like the seasons. He'd begun to atone for the deed in his past, had felt its burden begin to lift. The scream hadn't sounded in his ears for days. All of a sudden he thought of Ninnomi, the waif who'd helped to free him from his bondage to that memory, who herself was chained to the base Mr. Rudd.

Why shouldn't he free the girl in turn? He'd helped cast her into servitude six years back. He would liberate her now. He strode back inside and peered at her gentle features duplicated in wood. He would rescue her, and her great-uncle as well! He'd purchase them both from the vile eyeglass maker and bring them here, to his house, to live. He would speak to Mr. Rudd about it in the morning!

He looked long into the carving's eyes, communicating this promise.

The First Church's bell rang out four times. Hearing the sound, Mr. Hogwood whirled from the wig he was dressing, stormed toward the door, yanked it open, scouted King Street, and for the seventh time that afternoon failed to spy the hoped-for sight.

He stalked back to his bench. He snatched up his comb, but found it impossible to steady his hands. Madam Phipp's dinner would commence in two hours. All day his shop bell had tinkled gaily, announcing customers collecting their freshly dressed wigs for the affair. Day would shortly give way to dusk. The first of her guests would soon stride up her walk. And still no invitation had arrived!

Something passing the window caught his eye. He rejoiced, then found that what he'd thought was one of the widow's red-coated servants bearing a message was actually a bloody-shirted butcher hawking meat.

"Begone!" the wigmaker boomed, the order unheard by the butcher but noted well by his own apprehensive apprentices. Seething, he scolded his journeymen. He cuffed his know-nothing nephew, Dan. He kicked aside Charity, the cat, then swore at the sight of one of the legion of mice she was supposed to be catching. Draining his third mug of Malcolm's potent beer, he wondered if a rat hadn't drowned in the cask, spat, and roared for his manservant the requisite four times.

" 'Tis four o'clock!" he burst out in accusation, furious with himself for ever attending to the whelp's advice on wooing.

"Indeed, sir. We must soon be off. I've laid out your clothes for you in your chamber."

The wigmaker's brains, bubbling with yeast, strove to understand. "What say you?"

"Madam Phipp's other guests will arrive at six. As your invitation appears to have been mislaid by some dim-eyed scamp of a servant, you're not bound by that hour, and will pay her a visit in advance of the rest—and conquer her."

Mr. Hogwood's fleshy face twitched with hope.

"Through my own researches, I've discovered her chamber. The window to which may be easily gained by a hemlock tree close by."

The wigmaker gawked at his man. "Are you daft? I'm too old and too round to be shinning up trees!"

" 'Tis a time for bold deeds!" Malcolm declared. "One suitor will likely lead the woman from mourning to matrimony *this night*. Let the others trot tamely up to her door. Show her that you're a lion, not a sheep! That you mean to win her and will enter as you please! Your fiery resolve cannot help but throw a spark on the tinder of her heart." He paused. "As for the tree," he added at lesser volume, "I'll lend you a boost."

Confidently, Malcolm walked off. Mr. Hogwood, his wits soaked with the novice brewer's befuddling beer, felt a sudden, rapturous trust in the scheme. But what gift would he present to the woman? He couldn't hope to conquer her merely with the sight of his person. He wheeled and rushed toward the dining room.

He'd appealed in previous courtship presents to her stomach, her soul, and her heart, without success. This time he would appeal to her account book. He stood on a chair, reached for a sugar bowl high on a shelf, and climbed slowly to earth. It had been passed down through his wife's family, losing its top along the way. Still, it was a handsome piece: heavy, double-handled— and of silver. Here was the offering needed to ignite the affections of a merchant's widow! He polished it, begged his wife's forgiveness, returned to the shop, rooted about, placed the bowl in a mahogany box, then scurried to his chamber to dress.

A quarter hour later the wigmaker set off briskly toward Madam Phipp's. His scarlet coat matched the setting sun. He sported gold stockings and black silk breeches, and had carefully folded back his coat's cuffs to reveal his shirt's luxuriant lace. Twice his height and half his width, as if he were the same man rolled out thin, Malcolm followed two paces behind, bearing his master's gift. Wordlessly, he conversed with the several female acquaintances of his they passed, drawing upon a vast vocabulary of nods, winks, and smiles. Mr. Hogwood's eye fell on the males, checking wigs, clothing, and lace against their wearer's station in life, noting infractions to be reported, making certain that the hierarchy of man was written out plain.

They reached Madam Phipp's, slipped around to the side of the house, and halted before a tree. Mr. Hogwood studied it doubtfully.

" 'Tis a simple thing to scale," whispered Malcolm.

The wigmaker's breathing was made visible by the icy air. They passed in among the spokelike branches. The manservant set down the boxed sugar bowl and cupped his hands. "Place your foot here."

Mr. Hogwood did so, groaned mightily, all but snapped his servant's ten fingers, and stepped onto the tree's lowest limb.

"Note the great number of branches," chirped Malcolm. " 'Tis as easy as climbing a ratline."

Having never climbed one, or wanted to, the wigmaker failed to share his cheer. He grasped a limb above him with both hands, stepped up to a higher one with his feet, banged his head on a branch, heard the sound of cloth ripping, reached for his thigh, and found his palm was sticky with sap.

"And women delight in the scent of evergreens," Malcolm informed his master brightly. " 'Twill count in your advantage."

Mr. Hogwood ascended, finding the spirit to do so only by closing his ears to his manservant's encouragements. He sighted the window pointed out to him and scooted toward it along a limb, losing altitude as he went. He peered through the glass, found no one there, raised the window, tumbled inside, and moments later was handed his gift by the nimble-legged Malcolm, who quickly descended.

The wigmaker glanced around the room. It contained a canopied bed, a wardrobe, and a dressing table, and suddenly it occurred to him that his beloved might be unclothed when she found him, a circumstance that surely would *not* count in his advantage. Quickly, he set his box on her table. He searched his pockets, put a card on top, then noticed himself in her full-length mirror and was appalled to find that his trip through the tree had transformed him from a gentleman into a rustic. He plucked hemlock needles out of his wig, righted his hat, surveyed his torn breeches, strove to rid his hands of sap, then made out footsteps approaching and desperately dashed behind the bed.

Outside the window and one floor down, Malcolm leaned up against the house, ruminating upon his lot. He toiled for his master from cockcrow to curfew. He trailed him in the street like a dog. In church, he hunched on a bench in the loft with the other servants and slaves. Soon, however, his bondage would cease! Mr. Hogwood, thanks to Malcolm's coaching, would capture Madam Phipp's hand this night, the boldness of his master's entrance striking from her memory the lamentable gifts Malcolm had delivered. The wigmaker would move here after the marriage. Where, attended by her swarm of servants, he would find himself simultaneously with no need of Malcolm and greatly in his debt for the successful snaring of Madam Phipp—and would therefore gratefully set him free. The manservant trembled with bliss at the thought. Released from his indenture! A man among men! Sent into the world, as was the custom, with a new suit of clothes and his pockets full of shillings!

Craning his neck, he listened hopefully for sounds of progress from above. Then he heard a clang, turned around, looked in a window, and spied with surprise the serving girl he'd been pursuing. She was scouring an iron kettle. Malcolm tapped lightly, causing her to start, and pantomimed the raising of the window.

She shook her head strenuously. Undeterred, spurred on by her resistance, he undertook to impart through the glass his virtuous nature, his regimen of prayer, his deathless devotion to her alone, and the approaching date of his liberation.

Throughout this silent oration, Mr. Hogwood crouched in fear behind Madam Phipp's bed. She'd entered the room, her long body clothed in a gold satin gown, to his great relief. Her mood, however, had appeared so waspish that he'd hesitated to reveal himself. His knees aching, he listened as she lavished curses on some absent servant. Mumbling about her spectacles now, she consigned Mr. Rudd's soul to Hell, replied to herself that she'd spent good money on the maddening lenses, put them on, crossed the room, and glimpsed a reddish figure behind her bed.

"Giles! Whatever are you doing here?"

Mr. Hogwood, primed to proclaim his love, found his wits emptied of words.

"Stand up, squatting toad!" the woman commanded. "And while you're about, fling more wood on the fire!"

Dazed, the wigmaker straightened up. And gradually realized that between the failing light and her spectacles, the sight of his scarlet coat had enrolled him, in her mind, among her red-liveried servants, while his shape had fixed him as her stout footman, Giles.

"Be quick about it!" She struck him smartly on the hand with her folded, brass-ribbed fan.

The wigmaker winced and scurried toward the hearth. Amazed to find himself playing her lackey, wondering when to drop the disguise, he added two sticks of wood to the fire, hoping that warmth would improve her mood.

"Do you wish me to freeze? Pile the grate high!" She struck his knuckles. "Sag-stomached dunce!"

Mr. Hogwood massaged his throbbing hand. He stooped with a sigh, hoisted a massive log from the wood box, struggled to stand, then grimaced at a piercing pain in his back and dropped the log. It fell on the fire, sending a shower of cometlike sparks toward Madam Phipp's satin gown.

"Idiot!" she cried. "Cockle brains!"

Crouching on the floor, one hand on his back, Mr. Hogwood swatted at embers with his other, while Madam Phipp alternated between aiming her fan at the sparks and at him.

"'Tis ruined!" she raged. "Filled with holes like a cheese!"

Guiltily, the wigmaker rose, and found that a patch of sap on his elbow had affixed itself to the hem of her gown, which was now raised up to the level of her thigh.

"Knave!" Seizing the iron poker, Madam Phipp parted her gown from his arm with a blow to the latter which caused Mr. Hogwood to howl, slip, fall nearly into the fire himself, and to wonder why he'd ever praised her firmness with servants. "Saucy, impudent scoundrel!" she fumed.

She strode toward her wardrobe to select a new gown, then noticed the box on her dressing table. She took up the card that lay on top. " 'With the special compliments of Samuel Hogwood, wigmaker, King Street, Boston,' " she recited.

As if he'd just heard his entrance line read, Mr. Hogwood, eyes bright, climbed painfully to his feet and cleared his throat.

"What can that pompous little pumpkin want with me now?" she asked aloud. She whirled about. "Giles! See to it that the male servants' wigs are henceforth dressed at Mr. Swanton's shop!"

The wigmaker's words once again fled his mouth.

"And instruct the others to accept no further crushed oranges, foul-smelling books, battered lockets, or other endearments from Mr. Hogwood or his ill-bred man!"

The wigmaker's baffled brains churned in his head. *Crushed? Foul-smelling? Battered?* Then he knew. It was Malcolm who'd delivered each of those gifts! The rogue had opposed his courtship, fearing to be placed beneath a mistress so strict, and had cunningly led Madam Phipp to loathe him!

"Further," she barked, "make it known that the odious hair butcher is not to be admitted to the house!" She glared at Mr. Hogwood.

"Yes, Madam," he acknowledged, unable to free himself from his role. He turned his eyes from her. All was lost! The woman utterly despised him! He pictured the revenge he would wreak upon Malcolm. Then he thought of the gift within the box. Perhaps there was hope for him after all! The sight of silver might change her heart. He'd reveal himself, to her surprise and delight. She'd weep, pleading for his forgiveness. The sugar bowl, symbol of sweetness, would seal their vows to marry!

Mr. Hogwood approached. He cleared his throat and again readied his revelation. But before he'd a chance to speak his first word, Madam Phipp opened the box—and gasped. Her eyelids, hair, and body shot upward. She expelled a shriek that shook the windows. Openmouthed and mystified, Mr. Hogwood sprang forward, peered into the box, and found the freshly severed head of a mouse sitting in the sugar bowl.

"With Mr. Hogwood's *special compliments!*" the widow shouted out.

The wigmaker froze. It was Dan, his nephew! He'd repeatedly ordered his helpers to rid the shop of the heads Charity left. But only a scamp with Dan's shortage of wits would toss one into a box without looking!

"I'll see the fiend flogged for this!" raged Madam Phipp.

Mr. Hogwood, knowing his case was lost, backed away from the woman, then noticed her reach to remove her eyeglasses. Petrified now at being found out, unable to bear such embarrassment and fearful she'd scatter his brains with the poker, he flew toward the window, raised it, and leaped out onto the limb he'd entered by. His sudden weight causing it to snap, he plunged like a meteor onto Malcolm just as Madam Phipp's serving girl was tossing a pan of hot meat drippings on him—which sizzling liquid caused the tangle of arms and legs flailing in the snow to quickly divide nto two separate figures, who freed themselves from the fallen branch, frantically climbed to their knees, then their feet, then bolted down the walk and through the streets, furiously cursing each other.

Shortly past eight that evening, on Middle Street, a woman's scream slit the winter air. Mr. Trulliber, the night watchman, heard it and hurried his legs in that direction. Tut heard it and brought his eye down from the stars. Those who lived in the neighborhood cocked their ears, as if waiting for more. Those abroad in its streets and alleys stilled their feet, among them William.

He listened a moment, then continued on briskly. He'd been sent forth by Gwenne's royal command to find a raven's fallen feather, an all-but-impossible task at night. Seizing his chance to leave the house, he'd filled his pockets with scraps from the noontime feast and scurried out the door. Passing Dock Square, he'd turned toward Middle Street. It was a route he'd followed often of late. For the past three nights he'd slipped out the rear door after the Curries were safely asleep. Bringing what food he could to Michamauk, he'd stayed to receive from him in return the history and lore of their tribe. At the old man's request, then eagerly, he'd heard how Cautantowwit, the creator, had fashioned the first man and woman from stone, how a crow flew from his field with the first seeds of corn and beans and brought them to men, how the souls of the virtuous live in his house far away to the southwest. He heard of the deeds of the giant, We-tucks, and of Hobbomauk, the god who wandered at night, spreading evil and disease. Some of this he recalled from long before. But Michamauk had been a healer, a powwow, and on the night just past, once Ninnomi was sleeping, he'd told William things he'd never heard spoken, secrets meant only to be passed to a male: how to cure the sick, bring rain, see the future, how powwows of great power long ago could call mists into being at will, had caused water to burn and trees to dance. Fearing his knowledge would die with him, his great-uncle had kept him almost until dawn, burdened by how much remained to impart. The apprentice engraved all he heard in his memory. Though he'd lost Cancasset, his search for his brother had led him to happen upon Michamauk, who'd come to seem, over the course of these nights, nearly as important to him.

He marched through Middle Street's crusted snow. Shivering in the sky, all the multitudinous stars in the heavens were gathered, as if in public celebration of this longest night of the year. He passed a baker's, a hatter's, a hornsmith's, then halted at the sight of Mr. Rudd's. A crowd was clustered before his door. Lantern beams flickered and darted like fireflies. William stopped, thought of the scream he'd heard, then charged ahead.

"Outside, I pray you!" Mr. Trulliber bellowed.

A half dozen onlookers backed down the shop's steps. Slithering through the crowd like a snake, William gained a place near the front and managed to bend his head around the door. Three lamps sat upon the sand-strewn floor. By their light he beheld Mr. Rudd, on his back. His teeth were clamped upon a sheet of paper. His awl, the long cord of which still circled his neck, had been driven into his heart.

William's eyes froze upon the sight. Then he felt a hand on his shoulder, turned, and found Michamauk and Ninnomi behind him, their faces filled with fear.

"Read out what's upon the paper!" cried a voice.

Mr. Trulliber, anxious to study it also, was more anxious still to show that the examination of the scene was his own and would not be directed by spectators. He surveyed Mr. Rudd's workbench, then his tools, then his lamp, still burning. He pondered the footprints left in the sand. He stood before the hearth's hissing coals as if taking their testimony. Seemingly as an afterthought, he stooped, viewed the corpse, and tugged the paper from between its possessive teeth.

He lifted a lantern and glanced at the sheet. " 'Tis no more than an apprenticeship contract."

This news was digested, noisily, by the crowd.

Mr. Trulliber brought the page closer to his face. "With Mr. Rudd's own name written in as the apprentice," he added in puzzlement. His eyes traveled further through the form. "And 'eternity' given as the term of service." Apprehensively, he read further. "And with the master's name given"—he looked up—"as 'Satan.' "

William was aware of jostling behind him.

" 'Twas his tawnies!" yelled a woman.

The apprentice was startled to see two men wrestling with Michamauk. William vainly struggled against them.

"Murderous, devil-worshipping wretch!"

"To the gallows with him!"

"And the girl as well!"

The men pinned Michamauk's arms behind him. Ninnomi, frightened, attempted to flee and was snatched off her feet by a brawny blacksmith.

" 'Tis Mr. Rudd's redman, is it?" The watchman pointed his finger at Michamauk.

"Yes, sir!" came a shout. "And innocent of the crime!" The words had come from William's mouth.

Mr. Trulliber shone his light upon him. "And how come you to be so certain of this?" he skeptically inquired.

"The contract!" replied William. " 'Twas written upon. Yet neither of Mr. Rudd's Indians have been taught to hold a pen!"

Mr. Trulliber's doubtful smirk departed. Murmurs filled the air, as from a throng of restless dreamers.

"Perhaps *they* never learned to write," a voice commanded all ears. "But you have!"

William turned and found several lanterns trained on the fierce-eyed Mr. Baggot. Like a hovering hawk, the tithingman gripped the printer's apprentice with his gaze and sliced toward him through the gathering.

"In faith, your penmanship is peerless!" he praised him to his face. "As befits a boy of your *fine* education, tutored as Mr. Currie has seen fit. A lad who can con-

100

verse in Latin, read in Greek, and whose memory of Scripture mocks the town tithingmen's own."

Mr. Baggot smiled at his accomplished student. "But there's more to the boy!" he declared to the others. "He's a Narraganset, like Mr. Rudd's. Indeed, the three be related, I've discovered!"

Mr. Trulliber, who felt that discovering was properly in his domain, stared at the speaker disapprovingly.

"Mr. Rudd, as 'tis known, was not a soft man." The tithingman eyed Michamauk and Ninnomi. "His tawnies no doubt complained to their kinsman. The knave turned his villainous brains to the matter. And for four nights past has he lifted his gullible master's latch, as the redmen do well, and skulked through the streets to this very house—*with me following behind!*"

Astounded, William gawked at the man. His mind went utterly blank for a moment. He felt chilled, both from the cold and his fright. Then his senses returned, he reached into a pocket, and pulled out a heel of pumpkin bread.

"To keep them from starving!" he shouted out, holding it up for all to see.

"To plot the murder of an upstanding Christian!" the tithingman retorted.

A man stepped forward, lantern in hand. "Mr. Currie's William? 'Tis past belief!"

"Hell-hatched demon!" his neighbor disagreed.

Mr. Trulliber focused his eyes on a line at the bottom of the apprenticeship contract. " 'Sold by Charles Currie, printer, King Street, Boston,' " he read aloud.

Victoriously, Mr. Baggot eyed William. "Snared!" he proclaimed. "Just as I vowed!" He grasped the boy's arm with his shacklelike hand. "The serpent's shed his English skin, and shown himself a Satan-loving savage! Mr. Currie was lucky 'twasn't him murdered!"

The mention of his master widened William's eyes. "Pray, sir, let loose!" With a mighty tug, he freed himself from the tithingman, shot up the shop's steps, and asked to look at the contract for himself. By the watchman's light, he made out the line that Mr. Trulliber had just read out. The form had indeed been purchased at his shop. He studied the words that had been written in. The penmanship was not his. And though he didn't know whose it was, he felt suddenly certain that he'd laid eyes on the person. Hadn't he recently sold such a form, to a man so bundled he could scarcely be seen? A humming man, who'd peered strangely at William, as if in recognition?

"Enough! Seize the blood-drinking brute!" the tithingman ordered Mr. Trulliber.

"A moment!" William looked up from the contract and glanced about the eyeglass maker's shop. On one wall was posted a line of advertisements for the man's lengthy lineage of runaways. These too had been printed at Mr. Currie's. Scanning the row, his eyes halted upon a gap midway down the wall. He'd never heard of any of Mr. Rudd's apprentices being caught and returned. One of the notices had been removed.

"But of course!" he burst forth. " 'Twas one of the man's apprentices! I saw him myself, and sold him a contract just such as this!" He spun toward Mr. Trulliber. "Perhaps five days past! A thin man. His eyes green." He picked up a lamp, rushed over to the wall, and struggled to raise from his memory the name of the apprentice who'd scampered off between Jacob Fox and Samuel Stinchcombe.

"The boy speaks lies!" roared Mr. Baggot. "He only hopes to wriggle out of his noose. Watchman, to the prison with him!"

Mr. Trulliber, scowling at the meddling tithingman, ignored him on principle.

"Gideon Smeed!" cried William. "That's the name! I set the type for the notice myself!" He reached back into his memory. He faced the wall and shut his eyes. He tried to exclude all sound from his ears.

" 'Dashed off the eighth night of March,' " he recited. " 'His left print larger than his right. Both of them likely leading to Hell.' "

"Will the word of a sneaking tawny outweigh a tithingman's?" Mr. Baggot stormed.

"Clap the cur in chains!" boomed a man.

The apprentice appealed to Mr. Trulliber. "Surely you recollect Gideon! He'd seven toes upon one foot. For which cause Mr. Rudd swore he was fathered by the Devil and flogged him at his whim."

"And one night cut the lad full across his forehead with his awl," spoke a woman.

William recalled the low-brimmed hat the runaway had worn that day, so low it nearly rested on his nose.

"Of what import is this?" fumed Mr. Baggot.

103

"Suppose the boy be lying!" called a voice.

William looked back into the shop, then scurried toward the notices. He snatched from the floor a scrap of paper, eyed it, and gave it to Mr. Trulliber, who gravely studied it by his light.

" 'Twould appear to be a piece of a runaway notice torn from Mr. Rudd's wall. Containing the name of Gideon Smeed." The watchman raised his eyes from the scrap. "He likely hoped he'd be forgotten by snatching his notice. And was remembered instead."

William gazed upon Mr. Baggot. For the second time in a week his memory had thwarted the tithingman.

"Will justice be gulled by the boy?" the man raged.

"Silence!" demanded the watchman, drained of patience with Mr. Baggot. Determined to reclaim control of the proceedings, he tucked the scrap of paper in a pocket, then was struck by a thought. He turned and looked down at the eyeglass maker. His lantern trained upon the floor, he then slowly trod about the room, slipped from sight down a narrow hallway, and eventually reappeared outside the shop at the rear of the crowd.

"The boy speaks God's truth," Mr. Trulliber announced. "There's a trail of footprints left in the sand, with the left foot larger than the right. Plain to read as bear tracks beneath a bee tree. A trail that I warrant already leads out to the Neck and through the town gate."

William turned a triumphant smile on the stonefaced tithingman. Buzzing, the spectators began to disperse, carrying the news to their various hearths.

"But the rogue was abroad past curfew," Mr. Baggot thundered above the surrounding hubbub. "Surely he must be punished for that!"

The watchman approached him disdainfully. " 'Twas from mercy and therefore pardonable," he pronounced, from spite for Mr. Baggot and respect for William, who apparently was not one of the yawners, but was rather a lad who, like himself, could ignore the call of sleep, who knew the night. " 'Twas Mr. Rudd deserved to be punished, for ill-using his servants. As it appears he was. And as *you* shall be also should you not leave this matter to me, as is meet. To your bed, with the rest!"

Mr. Baggot glared at the watchman, then at William. Then he whirled furiously and stalked off.

Two onlookers chuckled. William watched the man vanish. Then he found Michamauk and Ninnomi and followed them to their shed. Their faces were glum.

"What will become of us now?" the girl asked William in Narraganset.

"I'm not certain," he answered her, soft-voiced. "Perhaps you'll be given to another master."

Michamauk shook his head. "No, Weetasket. Tonight we shall leave."

William's heart paused, then sped in compensation.

"Six years among the coatmen is enough. We're free tonight. Why should we wait and find ourselves slaves once more in the morning?" He lit a twig at his lamp and transferred the flame to his stone pipe. "Two days' walking west of our old home, I'm told, our people

105

can be found. Where Ninnomi will find a woman to teach her. And, later, a husband."

"You'll be caught!" spoke William. "Boston Neck is narrow. All must pass that way. And the guards at the gate will have their eyes open, looking for Gideon Smeed."

Michamauk seemed unworried. "I have also been told that the past four days' cold has frozen the Charles River." He puffed on his pipe and smiled. "Like the English soldiers, we will walk on the ice."

William considered. "But what will I do? I also have much more to learn. From you."

Michamauk stared at the apprentice. "Come with us."

T HE SUN ROSE with lordly splendor the next morning, searing the clouds and gilding the waters, driving the darkness before it toward the west, breaking the night's long siege.

At Madam Phipp's, the widow announced to her servants that Mr. John Sharpe, a shipowner of means, would shortly become their new master. Following this, she offered a curt apology to Giles, her footman, for her severity the previous evening, which repentance he accepted in bafflement. At Mr. Hogwood's, the wigmaker wasted no such contrition on Malcolm or his nephew, Dan, both of whom he'd belabored with a poker until the wounds to his arm, back, and hands inflicted by Madam Phipp had finally forced him to cease. Across Dock Square, Mr. Speke's door was rapped upon by Mr. Rudd's niece, who engaged the carver to build a coffin, adding the news that her uncle's Indians had apparently dashed off during the night. Silently, Mr. Speke wished them well.

At Mr. Currie's, the household was returned right side up. Sarah fetched the morning's water. James fed the fowls. Gwenne filled lamps. And William kindled the house's fires, his thoughts fixed on Michamauk and Ninnomi.

He pictured them walking toward the south, wished he were with them, wanted to show them that his success among the coatmen meant nothing. He'd often wondered to himself of late whether he'd return to his people if he could. Last night he'd had the chance. He'd declined. But it would come again, in two years' time, when he'd finished his term of service. When he'd be free to leave without being branded a runaway, another treacherous tawny, ungrateful to the warm-hearted Curries. Out of love and loyalty to them, he would wait. The craft he was learning beneath their roof in the meantime suited him, he reflected. He was a rememberer, a preserver, like the books and broadsides and tracts he printed. His nights with Michamauk, however, had led him to vow to devote his memory not to the Bible or the tales of the Greeks, but to the lore of his own Narragansets. He would listen and learn. He would become their book.

That night, once sleep had closed the Curries' eyes,

William slipped outside. Without setting foot in the street, where Mr. Baggot might be waiting, he crept through the snow to a house behind his own. Earlier in the day, he'd found the chance to speak with Thomas, the Narraganset man his father's age, who served there. He approached his quarters, set off to the rear. The air was chill. Above him, a maple's bare branches held a heavy crop of stars. Reaching into his waistcoat pocket, he drew out his bone flute and played three notes. And was admitted to the man's room, to listen.

NOTE

"A warr with the Narraganset is verie considerable to this plantation," wrote Emanuel Downing, in 1645, to his brother-in-law Governor Winthrop in Boston. "For I doe not see how wee can thrive untill wee gett into a stock of slaves sufficient to doe all our buisines."

The founders of the American colonies were accustomed to keeping servants. Old England was crowded with those who were willing to place themselves in service. In New England, however, where there was land for all, every man wished to be his own master. Indentured servants, who paid for their passage to America with their next several years' labor, were too few in number to fill the demand. Paupers and convicts were sometimes used. Slaves were imported from the West Indies. Desperate for help in their homes and fields, many of the colonists looked toward the Indians.

King Philip's War, fought thirty years after Mr. Downing's suggestion, left dozens of New England towns burned, and remains to this day, in its proportion of casualties to the general population, the bloodiest of America's wars. Civilians on both sides were massacred. It was a war of ambushes and midnight raids, a style of fighting favoring the Wampanoags, Narragansets, and Nipmucks who allied themselves, too late, against the English. Its largest pitched battle was the Great Swamp fight of December 19, 1675, a strike at the then-neutral Narragansets, whom the Puritans greatly feared. Brought on by more than the clamor for servants, the war did provide a supply of captives, some shipped to the West Indies as a commodity to be traded for African slaves, others serving in the colonists' homes. Though many of the help-hungry English saw the Indians as a providence, supplied by God to meet their needs, in practice they were found too intractable to make good servants. The colonists soon looked elsewhere.